SHEILA GATES

The Song of Rome Volume 1

A Time Travel Novel of Ancient Rome

First published by 8CATSBOOK 2024

Copyright © 2024 by Sheila Gates

All rights reserved. No part of this publication may be reproduced, stored or transmitted in any form or by any means, electronic, mechanical, photocopying, recording, scanning, or otherwise without written permission from the publisher. It is illegal to copy this book, post it to a website, or distribute it by any other means without permission.

This novel is entirely a work of fiction. The names, characters and incidents portrayed in it are the work of the author's imagination. Any resemblance to actual persons, living or dead, events or localities is entirely coincidental.

Sheila Gates asserts the moral right to be identified as the author of this work.

Sheila Gates has no responsibility for the persistence or accuracy of URLs for external or third-party Internet Websites referred to in this publication and does not guarantee that any content on such Websites is, or will remain, accurate or appropriate.

Designations used by companies to distinguish their products are often claimed as trademarks. All brand names and product names used in this book and on its cover are trade names, service marks, trademarks and registered trademarks of their respective owners. The publishers and the book are not associated with any product or vendor mentioned in this book. None of the companies referenced within the book have endorsed the book.

First edition

ISBN: 9798876562890

Contents

Foreword	iv
Preface	v
Chapter 1	1
Chapter 2	7
Chapter 4	18
Chapter 5	27
Chapter 6	34
Chapter 7	41
Chapter 8	44
Chapter 9	50
Chapter 10	57
Chapter 11	70
Chapter 12	76
Chapter 13	87
Chapter 14	94
Chapter 15	106
Chapter 16	118
Chapter 17	122
Chapter 18	129
Chapter 19	137
Chapter 20	150
Afterword	165

Foreword

One day ago I was a programmer, and one day later I actually traveled to Rome to become a Roman warrior.

Preface

Immerse yourself in the rich tapestry of ancient Rome, where political maneuvering, clandestine plots, and the insatiable pursuit of power take center stage. Sheila Gates weaves a gripping narrative that will transport you to a world of honor, deceit, and the struggle for the soul of an empire.

Dive into the heart of the Roman Senate, where Valerius Aurelius, a cunning and influential senator, finds himself entangled in a web of schemes and hidden agendas. As alliances shift and secrets are exposed, the fate of Rome hangs in the balance. Will the Song of Rome be one of triumph or tragedy?

Feel the intensity of the power struggle as Valerius Aurelius grapples with his ambitions, loyalty, and the consequences of his actions. Claudia Marsala, a woman of conviction, stands against the corrupting forces threatening the Republic. Can their choices shape the destiny of Rome, or will the city succumb to the shadows cast by greed and political machinations?

Brace yourself for a journey through the streets of Rome, where each step is laden with suspense, and every decision carries weight. The collision of ideologies, the clash of titans, and the unfolding drama will keep you on the edge of your seat, eagerly turning the pages to unravel the mysteries of "The Song of Rome."

Sheila Gates invites you to witness the grandeur and treachery of ancient Rome in this compelling tale that echoes the timeless struggle for power and the resilience of the human spirit. Are you ready to be swept away by the Song of Rome? Grab your copy now and embark on an epic adventure through the annals of history!

Chapter 1

The battlefield echoed with tumultuous noise—a cacophony of beastly roars and the crisp clash of weapons. In the distance, shadows of people were locked in a life-and-death struggle.

"Where am I?"

Henry struggled to open his eyes, only to be startled by the scene before him. This was clearly not a dream; he could feel the solid ground beneath his feet and the intense pain throbbing in his head.

Instinctively, Henry touched his head, finding it wet and sticky. Blood! The pungent smell of blood filled the air, permeating the entire arena.

Slowly sitting up, Henry surveyed his surroundings. The

sunlight was like a blade, too bright for him to keep his eyes open. Nevertheless, he could make out the vast circular arena and the structures within it.

"This is an arena!"

Henry was gripped with terror. The last thing he remembered was playing a game on his computer; how did he suddenly end up here? Had he really crossed over?

Surveying his battered body, Henry could hardly believe the harsh reality around him. He needed to find a way to survive in this brutal place.

Not far away, gladiators wielding daggers and small shields were engaged in combat. Henry, having studied Roman history, could confirm that they were Secutores.

These gladiators had already killed several fisherman-warriors around them and now turned their attention to a sword-and-shield fighter. Henry knew there was no mercy here; the only rule for survival was to kill or be killed.

With determination, Henry picked up a trident. At that moment, a Secutor lunged at him. Henry closed his eyes and thrust the spear with all his might. It pierced the opponent's abdomen, and hot blood sprayed onto Henry's face.

Henry trembled almost uncontrollably. The sudden brutality of the killing was too horrifying for him. Fortunately, the sword-and-shield fighter, aided by the fisherman-warriors, emerged

Chapter 1

victorious. Henry had narrowly escaped death, but the path to survival still lay ahead.

The joy of victory was quickly replaced by the harsh reality. Henry sat in a pool of blood, contemplating his escape. The wound on his head continued to bleed; he needed to tend to it to prevent infection. Searching the bodies, he found a piece of torn cloth and some freshwater to clean his wounds.

As night fell and silence enveloped the surroundings, Henry reflected on the proximity of life and death. Unable to sleep, the scenes of the recent killings replayed in his mind, and the smell of blood seemed to linger in the air.

Henry couldn't sleep. By the dim light, he examined the various wounds left by the battle. Multiple stab wounds, especially the abdominal injury, looked grim.

Henry needed medical attention and supplies, or his life would be in jeopardy. However, apart from the arena, he was clueless about this world.

The next day, Henry chose to stay amidst the ruins, searching for opportunities to survive. Perhaps, in the future, he could use his knowledge to become a healer or a teacher and leave this bloody place.

As long as he stayed alive, everything could change. Henry was determined to play to his strengths and continue his struggle for survival.

The Song of Rome Volume 1

Upon careful reflection, Henry finally realized—the owner of this body was named Gaius, a young nobleman.

Gaius's mother, Octavia, had an affair with a general, leading to his birth. Gaius's adoptive father, Marcus, harbored intense hatred for this non-biological son. Seeking revenge, Marcus arranged for assassins to kill Gaius.

However, the assassination only claimed Gaius's attendants, and Gaius himself escaped into the forest, eventually sold as a slave to the gladiator arena. For years, Gaius remained ignorant of his true identity, believing himself to be Marcus's son.

Now, Henry not only became a slave gladiator but also had the cunning Marcus as his enemy. A political feud and blood vendetta were converging with him as the target.

Locked in his cage, Henry contemplated, inadvertently catching the attention of a guard. Impatiently, the guard urged him, "Your master awaits."

Following the guard, Henry saw a familiar building—the Gladiator Training Academy. Unlike his expectations, the atmosphere here was not tense but filled with a solemn air of death.

A towering man approached Henry, a strict instructor hiding a faint smile. "You must learn to fight before the day is over. Tomorrow, your first match awaits."

The stakes of life suddenly escalated. Henry knew that he had

Chapter 1

to defeat his opponent in the arena to survive.

The instructor led Henry to the training ground, where various weapons—daggers, longswords, tridents—were scattered.

"Let's start with the basics," the instructor said, picking up a wooden sword to guide Henry.

Henry tried his best to follow the movements, but his body hadn't yet released its instinct for killing, clearly showing his unfamiliarity. The instructor grunted disapprovingly, "If you perform like this in the arena, you'll surely die!"

As the training concluded and the sun dipped low, Henry returned to his cage, exhausted. He knew he was far from ready to face his opponent the next day.

In the silence of the night, Henry pondered the life-and-death secrets of gladiators. Suddenly, a wounded comrade in the adjacent cage groaned in pain, his injuries still bleeding in the darkness.

Henry went to check and learned that this man was about to face the Grim Reaper in a battle. He realized that he, too, might face the same fate and shivered like a cold cicada.

The next day, Henry was brought to the center of the arena. Thousands of Romans in the stands cheered and applauded. He saw his opponent, a burly Gaul with a massive axe.

"Begin!" commanded the instructor. Henry reluctantly picked

up a longsword, advancing towards his opponent. Life and death hung in the balance on this day.

The crowd thirsted for blood, and Henry knew he had to win; otherwise, there was only one path—death. The mastery of battle would determine his life, and whether there was a possibility of a future…

Chapter 2

Weapons scattered across the training ground as Henry was summoned to the center by the instructor.

"Pick an opponent for the kid," the instructor ordered.

Gladiators around turned in unison, except for one towering figure who stepped forward—Septimus, the leader here.

"Looking for me?" Septimus chuckled, "This sprout is still green, a little force, and he'll snap."

The entire arena erupted in laughter, but only Henry deeply understood his current vulnerable position.

"Begin!"

Septimus roared, and a punch came straight at Henry. He narrowly avoided it but staggered back a few steps. Septimus, excited by Henry's agility, became even more thrilled.

The two engaged in hand-to-hand combat, with Henry using nimble dodges to evade Septimus's powerful punches. However, the stamina difference began to show, and Henry felt the strain.

"Stand and fight, be a man!" the instructor angrily shouted.

Taking advantage, Septimus landed a heavy punch to Henry's abdomen. Henry spat out blood and bent over in pain.

"Enough," the instructor intervened.

Henry lay on the ground, unable to get up. The crowd laughed and dispersed, leaving only Septimus, who loomed over him.

"Kid, the only rule for survival here is— the weak submit to the strong!"

Henry knew that without getting stronger, he was destined for a dead end. He had to relentlessly search for the source of strength or find an opportunity to overturn the fate of the weak.

Henry was thrown into a dark cell, enduring intense pain in his abdomen.

In the quiet of the night, Henry leaned against the wall,

Chapter 2

contemplating the scattered images flashing in his mind: a tall man shackling him into a carriage, and later, waking up in this place.

Had he once had a different identity? The surroundings were so unfamiliar; Henry was utterly lost.

Suddenly, a faint sound emanated from the adjacent cell. Henry looked over, witnessing a young prisoner gazing at him in the darkness.

"Like me, aren't you? In the life before coming here, we don't remember anything," the young prisoner calmly stated.

Surprised, Henry nodded, delighted to find a companion in shared amnesia. The young prisoner chuckled bitterly, "Here, everyone has lost their past. But now, only the strong can survive."

"So, how do you become strong?" Henry urgently asked.

"There's an old man here, a former gladiator. He can teach you the secrets of survival. But you must prove yourself and become his apprentice."

"I will!" Henry mustered the courage to accept. From today on, he could not afford to lose any opportunity. Overcoming adversity and becoming the strong survivor was his only way out here.

In the damp darkness of the cell, Henry asked the young

prisoner, "Where can I find this old man?"

The young prisoner pointed, "Tomorrow, you can see him in the mess hall. But remember, there's a constant danger to life here. You must be vigilant at all times."

The next morning, Henry arrived at the noisy mess hall. Everywhere, burly men stared at each other, and he was jostled by the crowd while looking for food.

At that moment, Henry caught a glimpse of an elderly man concentrating on his meal behind a pile of provisions. He determinedly pushed through the surrounding crowd and approached the old man, "Master, please take me as your disciple!"

The old man looked Henry up and down, seemingly testing him. In the midst of hushed whispers, Septimus, refusing to be forgotten, suddenly interjected, "This kid, he's just asking for trouble!"

Septimus scolded loudly and forcefully pushed Henry. Henry stumbled, crashing into the old man's food bucket. Grain scattered everywhere, creating chaos.

The old man stared at Henry beside him, a hint of disdain at the corner of his mouth. Henry knew that the path to survival was still long, and the crisis was subtly looming on the horizon.

Chaprter 3

Chapter 2

"Roar, roar, roar!" The audience collectively cheered.

Today's opponent was the tall and robust Gallic warrior, a Viking named Viking. He wielded a heavy hammer and wore thick armor, appearing exceptionally well-armored.

"This time, it's hopeless!" Septimus pounded his chest, "Just the two of us against that guy!"

However, Henry had made up his mind. "You handle the defense, and I'll take care of him."

"Begin!"

Viking came charging with the hammer. Septimus blocked the hammerhead. Meanwhile, Henry quickly used his dagger to slash at the opponent's exposed ankles.

"Hiss!" Viking cried out in pain, looking towards the sky. Henry took advantage and stabbed the other ankle.

Without his feet, Viking was suddenly handicapped. Septimus closed in, delivering powerful blows to the facial gaps.

With all their efforts, the towering gladiator finally fell to the ground, unable to open his eyes again.

"They won!" The audience exclaimed.

Henry breathed a sigh of relief. This victory was thanks to the application of historical knowledge and the coordination between the two, overcoming a formidable enemy. However, an even more challenging task lay ahead. After the battle, Henry and Septimus returned to the training ground. The old instructor watched, feeling sentimental.

"It's not easy for one of you to survive, and now not only coexisting but also cooperating, it's truly precious."

Henry and Septimus looked at each other and smiled. "We complement each other's weaknesses."

The instructor continued to ask, "How did you have such tactical insight? It's more seasoned than many of your peers."

Henry shook his head in confusion, still unaware of his past. The instructor left, pondering.

That night, Henry alone reflected on the past, and suddenly an unprecedented scene appeared in his mind—

A university classroom where he was demonstrating ancient military strategies. It dawned on him that he seemed to have been a historian?

The next day during training, Henry approached Septimus. With a trial-and-error attitude, Septimus offered to help him investigate his identity.

At that moment, a cry for help came from the adjacent cell. They rushed to see a new gladiator strangled to death in the cage. A larger conspiracy was brewing. Henry and

Chapter 2

Septimus squatted down to examine the body; the death seemed extremely unnatural.

"Someone wanted him dead," Septimus stated.

Henry suddenly noticed a tattoo on the inside of the victim's arm. "This tattoo looks familiar!"

Henry recalled that it was the emblem of an extreme populist student organization in his school. They advocated for discrimination against foreigners and supported a strict caste system.

"I remember now; I was trying to persuade them to disband this organization," Henry told Septimus.

The two reported to the instructor. The instructor was momentarily stunned but remained calm on the surface. "There are deaths here every day. Without concrete evidence, we can't draw conclusions. Continue your training."

After the training, Henry revealed his original identity to Septimus and the fact that someone had issued a kill order. Septimus frowned, saying, "This place is full of danger; we need to be even more careful in our actions."

The next day, Henry "accidentally" broke off a piece of iron bar in his cell and secretly handed it to Septimus. Septimus, without sleeping for a night, finally deciphered a code.

At this moment, a scream came from outside the cells. The two rushed to see, only to find another new gladiator had met a tragic end!

Henry and Septimus sought the newly deceased gladiator, hoping to gather more information. They saw the same tattoo on his hand. Henry sighed in dismay; did this person also hold some secrets when he was alive?

As they were investigating, the prison warden quickly arrived to clear the body. Henry negotiated quickly with him, and after reluctantly answering a few questions, the warden left.

"There is the same tattoo on all nearby victims; there must be something going on," Septimus pondered. "The warden also seems suspicious. We need to conduct a thorough investigation."

At night, Henry and Septimus sneaked into the warden's dormitory. After searching for a while, they finally found a secret logbook in a hidden compartment.

With torchlight, they discovered evidence that the warden was colluding with the extreme organization, plotting to eliminate certain gladiators.

"They want to manipulate order secretly here!" Henry exclaimed. As they discussed their next steps, patrolling guards discovered their smuggling operation and immediately rushed in.

Henry and Septimus had no choice but to put away the evidence and quickly withdraw. The road ahead was long; they had to

Chapter 2

find an opportunity to reveal the truth while staying vigilant not to be eliminated.

"Galba, Dubnillus, Boudicca, Octavius, Septimus, line up."

In winter, the Gladius Magnus Ludus gladiator school was assaulted by cold winds. The sun was washed white by winter rain, yet there was no warmth in the air. The gladiators were called to the training ground by the instructor Flavius.

In front of the training ground stood a three-story high Roman courtyard-style villa. The owner occasionally visited to watch the gladiator performances. However, these gladiators were slaves, without freedom, obligated to serve their masters without compensation.

"Today, as usual, pair up for training. Galba and Dubnillus, you are a team, Boudicca, Septimus, the two of you are a team."

After assigning training pairs, the instructor approached the new recruit Henry, resembling a teacher punishing a student from his childhood. Henry stood in the cold wind, feeling the turmoil and unease within.

Today, Henry was not placed in any training group. The instructor took out two "wooden swords" from the weapons arsenal, covered in rags. Henry had no idea what the instructor intended to do with him.

"Octavius, today, I will personally train you."

The head instructor, Artorius, a formidable Carthaginian, approached Henry. Henry felt a foreboding sense that the upcoming training would be brutal.

"Pick it up and come at me."

Artorius tossed two Roman short swords to the ground, leaving the gladiators in awe. Today's training seemed to be exclusively for Henry.

There was no escape for Henry. Artorius decided to shape Henry into a true bloodthirsty beast. Henry knew he couldn't just lie down; he had to treat his opponent as an enemy.

The battle began, and Artorius demonstrated a perfect blend of speed and strength, leaving Henry almost defenseless. Blood oozed from wounds, and Henry felt powerless and in pain.

"Get up. Stab me as if I were your enemy, as if I were a gladiator aiming to kill you. Kill me, you won't be held responsible; this is the master's command."

Artorius roared, the impact force intense. Henry struggled to stand up, and the two gladiators clashed again. Artorius no longer used weapons; he seized the short sword in Henry's hand with a crushing speed and then fiercely punched Henry.

In agony, Henry fell to the ground, hands covering the area where he was attacked. The instructor's foot pressed down on his head, and the training was far from over. This was the painful torment of a gladiator's growth, and the wealthy owner

Chapter 2

slowly entered the room—just the first lesson for the young gladiator.

Chapter 4

The roar echoed through the arena as Henry once again toppled a gladiator, another slave. The defeated gladiator trembled, pleading for mercy. Henry could see the fear and desperation in the young face, praying that Henry wouldn't strike him down, hoping the gods would intervene.

However, in the spectator stands, the Roman citizens and nobles seemed unwilling to let this gladiator live. Henry's swift victory over the poorly performing opponent didn't sit well with the audience. Waves of disapproval swept through the crowd, demanding Henry to end the defeated gladiator's life immediately.

"Sorry, brother."

The defeated gladiator knelt before Henry, who, despite a

Chapter 4

thousand reluctances, had to carry out the grim task.

The combat short sword aimed at the boy's throat, and Henry thrust it down forcefully.

In the next moment, blood spurted like a fountain from the shattered artery, splashing Henry's face. It wasn't Henry's first time killing a gladiator, but as a time traveler, such scenes were still too brutal.

Hope?

It was an elusive thing. Gaining freedom and glory from the arena was a deceptive illusion. Throughout the centuries, only a few managed to achieve honor and freedom in the arena, Spartacus being the exception. However, Henry, not being a legendary figure, considered such dreams too distant.

"Not bad, kid."

Descending from the arena, Henry, covered in blood, received warm embraces from his companions. The gladiator's world knew no mercy or sympathy; as long as you killed your enemies, gained glory, that was your ticket to survival and pride. Blood mixed with sweat, this was the realm of gladiators, a place for the pleasure of the aristocrats and commoners.

Agrippina, Julius's wife, intercepted Octavius, Henry, on his way to the cells. For a moment, Henry sensed something amiss. In the past few days, the lady of the mansion had looked at him not just with appreciation but with an undercurrent of something dreadful. What that was, Henry couldn't discern yet; after all, the thoughts of nobles were always more profound than those of commoners. Their cunning surpassed that of slaves, Spartacus being an exception.

"Thank you, lady. If there's nothing else, I'll return to the cell."

Enduring the overwhelming scent of perfume, Henry took a step back, creating distance from Agrippina. Enough for a face-to-face conversation but not uncomfortably close.

"Come back!"

Seeing her gladiator audaciously avoiding her, the elder noblewoman's anger flared. She forcefully pulled Octavius, Henry, toward her. In the emptiness, she pressed her lips, painted in fiery red, onto the young gladiator's.

Spit, spit, spit!

This moment left Henry feeling nauseated as never before.

But a slave was still a slave, utterly powerless to resist. Rejecting this old woman might mean enduring more torture in the days to come. Yet, not pushing her away would be disgustingly repulsive, losing his first kiss to a woman old enough to be his mother—such a feeling…

"What does this mean, lady?" Henry forced himself to speak, wearing an expression of confusion and unease.

Chapter 4

Agrippina looked at Henry, her eyes shimmering with a sinister allure. "Octavius, you displayed bravery in the arena, and I deeply admire your valor. How about becoming my personal guard? I will reward you with wealth and freedom."

Henry widened his eyes, and the turmoil in his heart intensified. Becoming a noblewoman's personal guard might seem like an opportunity, but in the world of aristocrats, relationships were complex, and surface glamour might hide endless conspiracies and dangers.

"Lady, I…"

"Don't worry, Octavius, I'll take care of you. Just fulfill your duties." Agrippina's voice carried a seductive tone, sending a shiver down Henry's spine.

Henry's mind was filled with complex thoughts, sensing the impending danger of being drawn into a vortex. Was becoming a noblewoman's personal guard an opportunity or a trap? The seemingly elegant woman before him concealed motives that were yet to be unveiled, and at that moment, Henry felt an unpredictable future looming ahead.

"Lady, I am still a slave. Why do you treat me so well?" Henry tried to clear his thoughts, searching for an opportunity to escape this predicament.

Agrippina's smile deepened as she leaned closer to Henry, whispering, "In this world, opportunities and traps are often closely intertwined, and I enjoy playing this game. Become my guard, and you will experience everything, whether it's glory and wealth or impending doom."

Her words were like delicate threads, entwining around Henry's heart. In this ancient and cruel Roman world, every step could become a sacrifice to fate. Standing at an unknown crossroads, Henry knew that no matter which path he chose, a heavy price would be paid.

She wore a purple gown, her black eyes resembling black pearls, and the deep collarbone outshining women of the same age. The noble demeanor and luxurious appearance attracted numerous Roman warriors and noble youths.

A playwright stood in Agrippina's room, composing a biography for this "young" noblewoman. The nauseating feeling overwhelmed Henry, and taking advantage of Julius being summoned to the Senate, Agrippina summoned Henry to her room, having these nauseating poets compose praises for her all day, demanding Henry to stay by her side.

To prevent Henry from resisting, she specifically called two guards to stand at the door. At any sign of disturbance, they would rush in to subdue the young gladiator.

Henry had no choice but to endure these absurd and tedious hymns and verses every day in this cell adorned with gold and silver satin.

"Listen, gladiator, if you don't sincerely obey me, I'll throw you into the underground arena to feed those wild beasts."

Chapter 4

The underground arena was undoubtedly one of those illegal arenas, similar to private clubs. There, the fighting was bloodier and more brutal. If the grand arena had some elements of performance, the underground arena was solely about survival.

There were no effective rules; the only goal was to kill the opponent. The audience mainly consisted of vagabonds and gamblers, uninterested in civilization and refinement. They only pursued the thrill of blood and flesh flying, along with dreams of getting rich overnight.

Thus, the bloodshed and violence in the underground arena were commonplace. Gladiators became even more ruthless there, but at the same time, those who managed to survive possessed highly advanced survival skills.

Henry understood all of this, but when this Roman noblewoman proposed such a disgusting condition, he resolutely chose the latter.

A man may be killed, not humiliated. A man should rather die in battle than submit to the bonds of a woman.

"Lady, if I must choose, I would rather die on my own battlefield."

With an unexpected courage, Henry spoke these words, even surprising himself. Perhaps after long battles in the arena filled with blood and sweat, an indescribable gladiator's spirit emerged within him.

"Do you really want to entrust your fate to those fierce and bloodthirsty beasts?"

Agrippina's thick and plump lips trembled again. Despite her gorgeous attire not enhancing her charm, adding a nauseating touch instead, Agrippina couldn't believe that the Octavius before her would make such a foolish choice. This elegant Roman noblewoman had witnessed the initial appearance of Octavius, the scared young boy who arrived at the gladiator school, like a panicked kitten, too scared to protest against any mistreatment. Agrippina couldn't believe that he had changed in just two months.

However, Agrippina was wrong again. Octavius was no longer the timid and fearful Roman noble youth he used to be but had transformed into another kind of man. Although initially, Henry feared this bloody world, two months of training were enough to bring about significant changes. The key was that Henry couldn't tolerate the disgusting requests of this Roman noblewoman.

"Yes, please allow it, my lady."

Henry stood to the side, continuing to answer respectfully. In the next moment, he witnessed Agrippina's face contorted in anger and her terrifying scream.

"Drag him down and feed him to the pigs!"

Agrippina finally erupted, and in the midst of the terrifying screams, Henry heard chaos, anger, and resentment from inside.

Chapter 4

No slave had dared to resist the owner's demands before; Henry became the first and the last. Agrippina wanted to send him to the underground arena, where the savages would tear him apart.

Destroy what you can't have. For the first time since arriving in this world, Henry felt the terror of a woman. Although not every woman was like this, Agrippina represented at least a part of them.

"You shouldn't have defied that woman. Do you know what the underground arena is? I crawled out of there, and you have no idea how terrifying it is."

Septimus approached, inquiring about Henry, who was about to be sent to the other end of the city. Two months of camaraderie had created a deep brotherhood between this robust Numidian and Henry. Watching his comrade pushed once again towards the abyss, Septimus's heart was undoubtedly filled with unease.

"Everything will be okay."

Henry intended to say more, but there were guards nearby, and some words were better left unsaid. After all, in this era, slaves had no rights, and if a noble wanted to kill you, it was as simple as lifting a finger. Agrippina was only sparing Henry's life because she believed this pretty face would change its mind. When he witnessed the bloodthirsty scenes of the underground arena, she assumed he would long to return to Gladius Magnus Ludus Gladiator School, continuing to be her secret lover.

But this time, Henry was determined not to turn back. Being insulted to death by a woman over forty was worse than being crushed to death by a barbarian in the arena.

"All right, brother. If you want to come back, I'll plead with the instructor and ask him to talk to the owner."

Septimus reluctantly released Henry's shoulder in the end. This peculiar Roman always brought surprises and amazement; his progress was too rapid, yet his thoughts were incomprehensible.

The last glow of crimson sunset lingered on the horizon, and Gladius Magnus Ludus Gladiator School, under everyone's gaze, saw Henry and a few gladiators convicted of severe crimes being stuffed into a prison cart, heading to another underground arena in the city of Rome. There, it was almost like entering another living underworld.

Chapter 5

"Beat him! Tear his bones off his legs!"

Blood, like red wine, spilled over the sandy ground of the arena as the furious Gauls and robust Egyptians wrestled. Septimus was right; the horror here surpassed Henry's imagination. It was a complete and inhumane slaughter, and the audience seemed to relish every moment.

The Gauls, holding the Egyptians from behind, engaged in a fierce struggle. Both sides were weaponless, perhaps having mutually disarmed each other earlier. Now, two equally savage gladiators engaged in a brutal brawl at the edge of the arena.

Amidst the maniacal cheers of the spectators, the Gaul lowered his head and ruthlessly bit off the Numidian gladiator's ear! The Numidian gladiator screamed in agony as the once black ear turned into a bloody mess. A large amount of blood gushed out from the wound.

The "victorious" Gaul bit into the ear, triumphantly holding it in his mouth. The audience erupted in celebration. Some gamblers, excited about their winnings, even threw coins at the Gaul who made the victorious gesture.

However, the fight wasn't over. As long as the opponent wasn't dead, the gladiatorial combat would continue indefinitely. That was the rule in the underground arena.

Just when everyone thought the Gaul had the upper hand, the Egyptian, who had just screamed in pain, suddenly charged forward. He forcefully pushed the Gaul, who was in the middle of celebrating, to the ground.

In the next moment, the robust Numidian gladiator extended his blood-soaked hands, clenched his fists, and unleashed a storm of blows on the fallen Gaul.

With his upper body pinned under the Egyptian, the Gaul couldn't move. The first punch almost blinded him, blood spurting from his eye sockets. Like a vibrant red corpse trembling under the savage Egyptian's fists, the Gaul gladiator convulsed continuously. It wasn't resistance; it was being beaten into a pulpy mess by the black gladiator.

A few minutes later, a large amount of blood, like a burst water kettle, poured out from the Gaul's body on the ground. It dyed the entire body of the Numidian gladiator. Only then did the audience realize who the ultimate victor was.

Chapter 5

In the astonished gaze of everyone, the Numidian ripped off the ear that the Gaul had bitten and delivered a final punch, disfiguring the Gaul's face beyond recognition.

Unlike the organized gladiatorial arenas on the ground, Henry, on the edge of the death arena, clearly saw the entire gladiatorial process. Rather than a gladiatorial battle, it was more like a massacre. Standing on the edge of the death arena, Henry experienced what Septimus had said – it was truly a hellhole, a blood-soaked abyss.

"Now, you will witness an epic duel – Octavius, the bull warrior from Gaul, and Maximus, the Gallian champion from Caledonia. They will engage in an epic battle here."

The Gaul's body was dragged away, leaving an empty space on the arena. The ground, covered with broken stones and fine sand, was stained with the blood of other gladiators. Without a doubt, these were the traces left after the gladiators engaged in two-on-two battles, judging by the blood splatters from all directions, showing how fierce the battles were.

Henry was pushed onto the platform of the underground arena. The handcuffs were temporarily opened, and there were only two weapon choices – a rusty sickle and a sturdy wooden stick.

After the host announced Henry's name, the entire arena erupted in mocking cheers. Obviously, Henry's physique was too frail, at least compared to the barbarians. How could such a gladiator withstand a punch from a barbarian like a bull?

Instantly, everyone placed their bets almost entirely on the subsequent appearance of the Caledonian.

"Now, cheer for our Caledonian beast."

Seeing Henry's frail frame, the host of the underground arena evidently didn't want to waste any more words on him. Instead, he directly shouted the name of the Caledonian gladiator – Maximus.

When the Gallian warrior entered the arena, the atmosphere ignited throughout the audience. It was a beast as robust as a bull. The Caledonian warrior was wrapped in armor, much like the heavily armed gladiators Henry had seen in the arena before. This beast's eyes showed no mercy or goodwill, only a thick intent to kill, as if it could only be satisfied in the blood feast.

The gladiators in the underground arena needed some packaging. The wealthy adorned their slaves with armor and shields, while the less fortunate ones, like Henry, had to be their own gladiators. In such cases, they could only choose from the meager selection of weapons available – in Henry's case, a wooden stick and a sickle. After the appearance of the Caledonian mercenaries, the host even took away the sickle, leaving only a rough, oversized wooden club.

Could a crude wooden club win against the bull-like man clad in iron armor? It seemed like a joke.

Henry felt somewhat speechless, yet the battle had to go on. In

Chapter 5

the underground arena, two entered, but only one could leave.

After the customary crossing of hands as a gesture of etiquette, Henry clashed with the Caledonian bull...

This was an inherently unfair fight. The Caledonian gladiator slammed Henry into the edge of the arena with his first charge, against a wall stained with blood.

The overwhelming force had already completely overwhelmed Henry before the match even began.

The space for combat in the underground arena was limited, comparable to a modern boxing ring. Unlike the circular arenas on the surface, there was no open ground for the gladiators to run and jump freely. Here, combat relied more on brute force than agility.

"Come on, little fresh meat."

Stimulated by the frenzied cheers of the audience, the Caledonian gladiator became even more excited. The seemingly feeble Roman in front of him was nothing more than a trembling chunk of meat in his eyes, a chunk of meat quivering under the blade.

"Roar."

The barbarian roared and lunged forward, but Henry nervously evaded. The Caledonian gladiator's assassination attempt fell short. Henry appeared behind him, raising the wooden stick to strike down with force. A dull thud echoed from the helmet – the sound of the wooden stick hitting the iron armor. If it were a double-edged sword, it might have severed the loosely secured helmet, but in Henry's hands was a mere wooden stick.

No matter how mighty the stick, it couldn't shatter an iron helmet. Did he think he was a Germanic kid?

The back of the Caledonian gladiator's head took a hit, and the helmet trembled but didn't fall off. Yet, the barbarian turned around and charged toward Henry.

Henry retreated, trying to maintain distance, but the Caledonian beast's speed and strength made it nearly impossible for him to evade. Every swing of the wooden stick was effortlessly avoided by the ferocious adversary, exposing Henry to an even more dangerous position.

The audience started to jeer, shouting support for their favored gladiator. Henry's situation became increasingly difficult, and the hefty wooden stick in his hands seemed utterly useless. The arena walls were close behind him, with no space to leverage for evasion.

Suddenly, the Caledonian gladiator sidestepped, quickly turned around, and aimed a powerful blow at Henry's waist. Henry tried to dodge, but he was still hit by the opponent's iron fist. The immense force transmitted through him, making him feel as though he'd been struck by a war chariot.

"It seems like this match isn't very exciting!"

Chapter 5

The host mocked, and the audience cheered in delight. Henry felt despair creeping in; his body was starting to give in, while the Caledonian beast remained full of strength, launching relentless attacks.

At this moment, Henry suddenly recalled some combat techniques Septimus had once taught him. He knew he couldn't continue passively taking blows; otherwise, this gladiatorial battle would soon be over.

Witnessing the Caledonian gladiator charge again, Henry executed a sudden forward somersault, avoiding the opponent's fierce strike. Simultaneously, he swiftly grabbed a handful of sand from the ground, throwing it into the opponent's face. This brief gap allowed Henry to catch his breath, but the Caledonian gladiator angrily rubbed his eyes, quickly recovering.

The situation once again turned against Henry. The barbaric opponent grinned, seemingly carefree yet exuding wildness and cruelty.

Henry knew that if he didn't quickly find an opportunity to change the tide, this would be his final battle. In the spectator stands, gamblers eagerly prepared to claim their winnings.

Chapter 6

"You actually threw my gladiator into that filthy, disgusting underground arena?!"

Upon returning home, Julius launched a stern reprimand at his whimsical wife. For Julius, a man of immense wealth, the outcome of a gladiator was not a significant matter. What he couldn't tolerate was his wife's unauthorized disposal of his property, including those gladiator slaves considered noble assets.

"He requested it himself," Agrippina, sitting on the edge of the bed, responded indifferently. Traces of wine lingered on her lips, evidently indifferent to her husband's anger. The arrogance of the noblewoman manifested even more at this moment.

Julius roared, "You had me followed!"

Chapter 6

This shout completely caught Agrippina off guard. She realized that, when alone at home, Julius had already arranged for someone to monitor her every move. In Agrippina's perception, this husband had always been a weak and declining noble, and she had not guarded against such actions.

"I not only had you followed but also had them watch your servants. I know everything about your past actions, every move you've made. From now on, everything in this house is under my command, including all the property. Without my permission, don't think you'll touch a single coin."

Julius finished speaking, and a resounding slap landed on his face. The man's cheek turned slightly red, symbolizing his past incompetence and the moment Julius confronted his wife. Henry was just the catalyst for this family dispute; even if Agrippina hadn't sent Henry to the underground arena, Julius would have found another way to expose this hidden truth.

"Who do you think you are? Relying on your father's support, thinking you can tower over others? From now on, everything in this house is under my rule. Your father's support, whether given or not, doesn't matter. I'll send guards to watch over every passage in the house. If you want to go out freely again, come beg for my mercy first."

Julius grabbed his wife's wrist, roaring. At this moment, Agrippina couldn't believe her husband possessed such determination to resist her authority. Inside the house, the argument between the two spilled out, making the guards nervously stand at the door, unsure of what to do.

"Roar."

Amidst the barbaric collision, Henry once again dodged his opponent, closing the distance to just a meter. In the next second, he launched a fierce attack, the short sword thrusting towards the barbarian's thigh. Seizing this brief opportunity, Henry swung the wooden stick forcefully, sending the Caledonian gladiator to the ground. Blood gushed from his mouth, but Henry knew it wasn't enough to end the fight.

The barbarian rose again, and Henry raised the wooden stick, aiming for the head. However, the heavy iron armor lessened the damage, only momentarily throwing the opponent off balance. For Henry, it wasn't sufficient.

As the barbarian attempted to rise again, Henry didn't give him a chance. He reversed his grip on the dagger, swiftly stabbing towards the chest. This thrust went straight to the heart, the only unprotected area under the barbarian's entire iron-clad body. The fight ended within a short time, and the arena fell silent until the voices of a few cheering commoners loudly shouted Henry's name – Octavius… After the battle, the underground arena fell into a moment of silence. The audience members who had bet on the Caledonian fell silent, while those supporting Octavius (Henry) rejoiced. This outcome was unexpected for the majority.

Henry stood in the arena, the dagger plunged into the sandy ground, scanning the surroundings. Disappointed faces and resentful glares from those who lost their bets, mixed with the cheers of those who were fortunate, interwove in the crowd.

Chapter 6

"Octavius! Octavius!"

The victorious cheers came from some corners, and a few people began to celebrate. However, the rules of the underground arena were cruel and clear: only one could leave alive.

Henry looked at the barely alive Caledonian gladiator. Despite defeating his opponent, he knew his victory wouldn't allow him to leave this bloody arena. It was the rule of the underground arena – defeat your opponent to stay, and every gladiator's goal was survival.

The gleam of the dagger reflected in Henry's determined and resolute eyes. He wasn't satisfied with becoming entertainment for the spectators in this barbaric game; he had bigger goals, loftier ideals.

The audience reentered the tense atmosphere, uncertain about what would happen next. Henry's fate in the underground arena remained uncertain, but his inner determination was enough to find a way out in this brutal environment.

Back at the noble mansion, Agrippina faced Julius with gritted teeth. She hadn't anticipated her husband's resolute resistance, revealing a long-hidden assertiveness. The entire mansion seemed to undergo a seismic shift in an instant as Julius shed his past image of weakness and emerged more determined.

Julius coldly gazed at his wife, regaining control of everything. This night, he was no longer the weakling of the noble mansion but had reclaimed dominance over the family.

"You thought you could manipulate me, but from now on, I call the shots in this household. I'm well aware of all your actions. If you dare to cross the line again, the consequences will be dire," Julius spoke with determination and a warning tone.

Agrippina felt a mix of anger and helplessness at this unexpected turn. She couldn't fathom Julius having so many means at his disposal, nor did she expect him to be so decisive at this crucial moment. Faced with her husband's threats, she found herself in an unfamiliar and dangerous situation.

"Do you think this is the end? While you tidy up everything, let me tell you, our story is just beginning," Agrippina, though in retreat, silently vowed in her heart that she wouldn't back down. A more complex and intense struggle was about to unfold.

Inside the mansion, guards were tense and vigilant. Julius stepped out of the bedroom, reasserting control over the entire mansion, while Agrippina remained in what used to be her domain, her eyes revealing concern for an unknown fate.

In a corner of the underground arena, Henry was forced to stay behind, facing unknown challenges. The dagger still gripped in his hand, his determination grew stronger. Perhaps it was a narrow stage, but he was determined to write his own legend on this bloody soil.

As night fell, the noble mansion and the underground arena became intersecting points of two different worlds. Julius rose in political maneuvering, Agrippina held her ground in

Chapter 6

resistance, and Henry sought a way to survive in the brutal arena. The stories in this ancient city would gradually unfold in the depths of this night.

In the underground arena, Henry persisted in his struggle against the burly Gaul until Roman guards stormed in, forcibly separating them. Henry's heart surged with wildness and a thirst for freedom, his eyes gleaming with unwavering determination. Even as they were torn apart, his tumultuous emotions remained difficult to calm.

The Roman guards, messengers sent by Julius, approached Henry, demanding his return to the gladiator academy. Henry didn't resist because he understood that evasion was a dead end. In the underground arena, he had learned the rules of survival. He was no longer the slave trapped in the noble mansion; he had become a formidable gladiator.

"Octavius, the master wants you back."

The lead Roman servant spoke arrogantly, and Henry nodded in silence, following the guards out of the underground arena. The burly Gaul lay gasping on the ground, having become the prey of the arena, while Henry, on his way back to the academy, harbored new plans in his heart.

Returning to the gladiator academy, Henry faced Julius's smile and sensed the authority of his master. However, his inner self was no longer the weak and submissive one of the past. He knew that survival in the underground arena was not just to please the nobility but to seek strength and opportunities, to change his own fate.

As the gladiator academy's convoy headed towards the school, Julius's servants briefed Henry on the upcoming grand gladiatorial competition. This event featured not only beasts but also team-based battles, promising an entertaining and thrilling spectacle. Henry found himself temporarily added to the roster, becoming one of Julius's strongest teams, attracting attention from the crowd.

In the noble mansion, Agrippina faced loneliness and frustration. Once a lofty noblewoman, she had overnight become a tool of revenge for her husband. Julius used his power to strip her of everything, yet it also ignited a flame of resistance deep within Agrippina. She vowed to reclaim her status and dignity, and perhaps this upcoming gladiatorial competition would be her chance to challenge destiny.

Under the early summer sun, the fate of Rome intertwined in the underground arena and the noble mansion. Julius and Agrippina engaged in political strife, while Henry sought freedom in the bloody arena. The impending grand competition was destined to be a new storm in this ancient city.

Chapter 7

In the heart of the Roman Empire, the Colosseum teemed with spectators, creating an atmosphere of fervor. Nobles adorned in extravagant attire sat on lofty tiers, overlooking the gladiators below. Commoners crowded the lower tiers, cheering and shouting for the gladiators' combat.

Cups filled with red wine were brought to Agrippina's lips by a servant. She sipped gracefully, then turned her gaze to the arena. Today, she would witness a grand gladiatorial performance.

Julius and Valerius Aurelius sat side by side in the stands. Both were senators of the Roman Senate and staunch supporters of the Triumvirate.

"Julius, I heard you've sent out your most elite gladiators for today's matches?" Valerius Aurelius inquired.

"Not the absolute elite, but certainly not the worst," Julius replied nonchalantly.

They exchanged a knowing smile. Both understood that this gladiatorial contest was not just entertainment; it was a political maneuver.

The first match commenced. Four gladiators armed with weapons entered the arena. Their opponents were two ferocious lions.

The lions roared and charged at the gladiators. The gladiators wielded their weapons, resisting with all their might. However, the lions' strength was overwhelming, quickly subduing the gladiators.

The two lions brought the gladiators down, tearing and biting into their bodies. Blood splattered, and screams echoed throughout the Colosseum.

The audience held their breath, watching the carnage unfold. They cheered for the gladiators' bravery and applauded the ferocity of the lions.

Julius and Valerius Aurelius exchanged a glance; they knew the gladiatorial spectacle had achieved the desired effect.

The subsequent matches grew even more brutal. Gladiators were mauled by wild beasts, burned alive, and impaled by blades. The spectators' emotions heightened, cheering for the gladiators' deaths and getting excited by the spurting blood.

Chapter 7

Satisfied, Julius and Valerius Aurelius observed it all. They understood that the gladiatorial games had successfully diverted people's attention from political struggles, immersing the Roman populace in bloody entertainment.

After the gladiatorial games concluded, Julius and Valerius Aurelius left the Colosseum. They knew their mission was accomplished.

On the way home, Julius said to Valerius Aurelius, "That gladiatorial contest was truly magnificent. It made the Roman people forget all their troubles, immersing them in bloody entertainment."

"Yes," Valerius Aurelius concurred, "this gladiatorial contest was not only a spectacle but also a political victory. It successfully shifted people's focus away from political struggles, solidifying the Triumvirate's rule."

Julius and Valerius Aurelius exchanged a proud smile, aware that they had firmly secured control over Rome, and no one could shake their position.

Chapter 8

In the heart of the Roman Colosseum, twenty gladiators from the Julius family stood side by side. Clad in armor and wielding weapons, they awaited the imminent battle.

On the opposing stands, fifty thousand Roman citizens erupted in cheers, excited for the upcoming gladiatorial spectacle.

"Brothers, today, we face a team gladiatorial contest. Only through unity do we stand a chance to emerge victorious. When we enter the arena, follow my commands, and let us fight as one," Septimus, the commander of this gladiator squad, declared loudly.

Henry stood in the midst of the group, absorbing the primal and exhilarating roar from the Roman citizens. It was the collective voice of fifty thousand people, resembling a storm.

Chapter 8

Fear?

That had become a thing of the past months ago. As gladiatorial combat transformed into a profession, Henry found himself, like all gladiators, devoid of fear for blades, blood, or injuries. It was now about bravely facing enemies until the end of the arena battle, with victory as the ultimate goal.

The iron gates of the arena swung open, and all gladiators, driven by their desire for blood and glory, entered the largest slaughterhouse in the Eternal City—the Roman Colosseum!

"Ladies and gentlemen, friends from Rome who have come from afar, today, we are here to host a magnificent and grand competition. This is a spectacular event commemorating the final battle of Rome against Carthage—the Battle of Zama. Now, standing before us, is the formidable and savage legion of African warriors led by the infamous Hannibal—the African Conquerors!" The enthusiastic announcer proclaimed, stirring up the atmosphere.

In response to the significance and story narrated by the contest, the Roman audience, now aware of the enemy they faced, began hurling objects towards the center of the arena, expressing their disdain. Boos echoed throughout the stands.

Standing in the middle of the squad, Henry knew that the audience's intense hatred for Hannibal stemmed from the fact that this Carthaginian general had almost single-handedly annihilated Rome. A whole generation of Romans perished in the Roman-Carthaginian wars, known as the Punic Wars. If not for Fabian tactics later employed by Rome, the city might have succumbed to Carthage. Hence, the Romans harbored deep-seated resentment towards Hannibal.

"Quiet down."

Seeing the tumultuous atmosphere in the spectator stands, the arena's host knew it was time to introduce the teams ready for slaughter.

"Now, welcome our most powerful, most valiant, and epic legion of victors—the Roman legion led by the African Conqueror Scipio!" The announcer's thunderous voice resonated, intensifying the fervor in the arena.

As the host passionately called out, the audience's cheers became a rhythmic and organized roar, akin to thunder before a storm.

And indeed, this gladiatorial spectacle was a storm.

When the five large iron gates of the Roman Colosseum simultaneously opened, the twenty gladiators from the Julius family on the field could hardly believe their eyes! This closing match was not a gladiatorial contest; it was a massacre.

"Julius told us it's a team gladiatorial contest."

Plenius, one of the gladiators, couldn't help muttering. Instead of gladiators, the figures appearing on the field edges were regular Roman soldiers! Clearly, this event was merely

Chapter 8

a performance orchestrated by politicians to entertain the audience and justify launching a war against the barbarians. This grand display aimed to support Caesar's conquest of Gaul. Everything was planned in advance, but Septimus and all the gladiators entering the arena were unaware, and even Henry was oblivious.

"Damn, that schemer deceived us."

Fabius roared in anger.

"Not necessarily; perhaps the master is also unaware."

Compared to the others' resentment, Septimus spoke up in defense of Julius. Having fought for the Julius family as a gladiator for a decade, Septimus knew his master was not someone who went back on his word. It was possible that this time, Julius had also been deceived.

"You tell me this is a team competition, but what is this now?"

On the stage, Julius had quietly approached the smug host from behind, gripping the arena host's hair like a frustrated wild beast, angrily questioning. Septimus, Plenius, Fabius, and the other twenty gladiators were the elite of the Julius family, the entire arsenal of the Gladiator Academy. Yet, this damn conspiracy sought to execute these twenty innocent gladiators to please the Roman populace, orchestrated by politicians—a shameless act.

But Julius was helpless because conspiracies always required sacrifices, and Julius had already sided with the Triumvirs. This gladiatorial contest itself was a stage set by the Triumvirate. If Julius expressed dissatisfaction, his collaboration with Pompey would come to an end. Julius seethed with anger, regretting his past alliance with the Triumvirs. There are no free lunches in this world; Pompey might have given Julius benefits, but it was akin to handing him a vulnerability. And this, Julius was still unaware of before the gladiatorial contest started.

"Brothers, now is not the time to argue right or wrong. The enemy is right in front of us. Unite, fight together, and we may still have a chance. If we keep complaining, we'll truly become sacrificial lambs in this conspiracy."

Seeing unrest within the team, Henry couldn't help but step forward. Public speaking was not originally Henry's forte; back in college, the introverted guy stumbled through every speech, nervously stuttering. However, in this world of ancient Rome, where survival required shedding his former timid habits, Henry had to adapt.

Unexpectedly, Henry's words had a profound effect. The gladiators began rallying together, searching for potential breakthroughs in this battle.

The Roman legion was a regular army, not newly formed. It seemed these soldiers were seasoned veterans. Septimus had once served in the Numidian-African Legion, giving him some understanding of legion tactics. Henry, having read about Roman legion tactics in books, was somewhat mentally prepared for what lay ahead. However, the other gladiators in

Chapter 8

the team were caught off guard by what might unfold next.

Chapter 9

"Left! Left!"

Septimus shouted as Roman infantry hurled heavy javelins from the left flank.

The gladiators quickly raised wooden shields for protection, but some javelins pierced through, lodging in the gladiators' hands, impossible to pull out. Blood spurted like a fountain, staining Plenius and Fabius' left hands red; evidently, they had lost their combat effectiveness.

"Attack formation, advance!"

A Roman centurion bellowed, and soon, a Roman squad of forty assembled into a neat formation, advancing toward the gladiator team.

Chapter 9

The situation was dire. Henry knew this was the most formidable infantry formation in the ancient Roman world. In the battlefield, a Roman legion's infantry formation comprised eighty men, but in the arena, it couldn't accommodate so many Roman soldiers. Furthermore, the gladiator team had only twenty members. If the Roman regular army was too numerous, the spectators would accuse them of bullying the few.

"Septimus, tell everyone to disperse. You and I will charge from both flanks, aiming for their calves and heels."

After closely observing the situation, Henry devised a strategy. It was the only way to break the Roman phalanx. The castle attack formation involved soldiers closing their shields together, forming an impenetrable shield wall, then advancing toward the enemy. This defense could effectively withstand attacks from the front and diagonally above. However, due to the size limitations of Roman legion shields, they couldn't cover the ground, leaving the Roman soldiers' calves and heels exposed. Henry seized this vulnerability, yelling at Septimus.

Septimus quickly understood his comrade's intent. Gripping sharp swords, Septimus and Henry charged from the flanks, aiming for the well-organized Roman phalanx.

A breathtaking scene unfolded.

On the field, all the Julius family gladiators dispersed instantly, leaving the legion without a clear direction of attack. Septimus and Henry had already sprinted to the flanks. Just before colliding with the phalanx, Septimus swiftly slid to the ground, his sharp gladiator short sword reflecting a chilling white light.

All Roman soldiers assumed this foolish gladiator would face them head-on. But in the next second, Septimus dropped low, his Roman short sword turning into a cutting machine. As it swept across the flank of the legion, it injured the heels of four or five Roman infantrymen. With Henry on one side and Septimus on the other, they managed to knock down seven or eight Roman heavy infantrymen.

"Phew."

The sudden bloody spectacle made the audience forget the roles these two teams were playing. The commoners began cheering, rooting for the gladiators.

…

"What's going on?"

Members of the Brutus family in the stands began questioning the arena host. This was supposed to be a slaughter of gladiators, a promotional event glorifying legion supremacy. But now, the situation had turned, and the gladiators were gaining the upper hand. Even the commoners were cheering for these two gladiators. At this rate, the original intent of the match would be lost. It was a waste of resources.

"Uh, this is just an accident, dear Brutus."

Chapter 9

Facing the inquiry from Roman nobles, the arena host stammered, unable to answer. In his heart, he hoped the damn Roman soldiers would quickly rise to counterattack and kill these troublesome gladiators.

"Roar."

Once again, the gladiators' roars echoed on the field. After Septimus injured the ankles of four Roman heavy infantrymen, he charged into the heart of the phalanx while the Roman infantry was still regaining their footing. Then, the feast of slaughter commenced.

Seizing the opportunity, Henry rolled into the formation, penetrating the heart of the phalanx. Two gladiators wielding dual blades, one by one, severed the throats and pierced the abdomens of Roman soldiers.

The sudden eruption of blood turned the atmosphere in the spectator stands electric. All commoners stood up, involuntarily shouting, "Kill, kill, kill."

The atmosphere on the scene escalated step by step.

"Ah!"

Before the legion formation could adjust, Septimus took down the last legion infantryman, then left the phalanx amidst Henry's loud shouts. After all, two against thirty were unfavorable odds, and if the phalanx cleared an area, allowing legion infantrymen to engage freely, Henry and Septimus would be at a disadvantage.

The legion formation had to change its formation temporarily. Everyone lined up, facing the gladiators directly, preparing for a head-on confrontation.

This was the scene Henry wanted to witness. Once the Roman legion infantry formed a straight line and engaged the gladiators freely, these Roman soldiers would be no match for the gladiators. Gladiators fought one-on-one in the arena, and in a one-on-one fight, legion infantry was at a disadvantage.

"Brothers, let them witness the faith of the gladiators! Courage and honor, brothers!"

After killing eight Roman infantrymen, Septimus returned to the gladiator team, shouting slogans loudly. The morale of all the gladiators present was boosted to the extreme. The next moment, the fifteen Julius family gladiators collectively roared, launching a beast-like assault on the enemy.

In the blink of an eye, this section of the arena in the grand colosseum turned into a pool of blood, a place of slaughter.

With the cover of his teammates, Henry charged fiercely towards a Roman heavy infantryman. Using the shield as a stepping stone, his robust body leaped high. In the terrified gaze of the Roman soldier, the gladiator's short sword pierced through the Roman heavy infantryman's throat, and crimson blood instantly splattered the sand.

Chapter 9

The Roman citizens in the stands, whether commoners or knights, cheered wildly for the gladiators' blood-pumping performance. The names of Hannibal and the African Legion were forgotten, discarded in favor of the brutal and bloody spectacle. At this moment, only the visceral satisfaction of witnessing carnage could satiate the audience's visual cravings.

"Roar."

Another strike. Henry precisely thrust the short sword into the mouth of a Roman infantryman. A wave of warm blood splattered across his entire body. Half a year ago, he was a gaming recluse, but now he had transformed into a god of war. Henry could no longer adapt to this change in character, often getting immersed in this cruel and blood-soaked world, forgetting his identity from his past life.

In the end, only two trembling Roman infantrymen remained on the edge of the arena. They had come to participate in the match, but now, they had become the targets of this group of beasts. The pitiable legion infantrymen didn't care about honor or rewards anymore. They just wanted to be let go. However, that was impossible. At this point in the battle, the audience had gone mad. Releasing the legion infantrymen now would provoke strong resentment from the Roman commoners. Doing so would undoubtedly deviate from Caesar's initial purpose in hosting this event.

Thus, the unfortunate Roman legion infantrymen could only be cornered, waiting for the gladiators' final slaughter.

"Kill, kill, kill!"

On the field, the storm-like shouts resonated again. Fifty thousand Roman spectators on the stands collectively roared, the scene and momentum making the gladiators' blood boil. This was their purpose in coming here – to fight for glory and freedom! Without a trace of mercy, Septimus thrust the short sword into the throat of the last Roman infantryman.

The gushing blood drove the audience into a frenzy. This was the most spectacular performance they had ever witnessed in history. Even after the battle, they would still thank Caesar for his generosity and selflessness. However, they had forgotten Caesar's true purpose. They cheered for the gladiators' blood-pumping display, overlooking the fact that Caesar aimed to rally the support of the Roman commoners and knights for his campaign in Gaul.

And after this battle, Henry not only became a hero among the Julius family gladiators but also an idol among the Roman commoners.

Chapter 10

Becoming famous wasn't always a cause for celebration, at least not in the Roman society. After the grand slaughter in Caesar's arena matches, winning countless glories, Henry felt everything was becoming unbearable. Roman women surrounded him like flies, sniffing at the scent on him, touching every muscle of the champion gladiator.

It was an appalling feeling. While other gladiators might enjoy such scenes, Henry was not accustomed to it. The overpowering perfume of those Roman women suffocated him, yet he had to attend various banquets with Julius.

"Julius, in two months, the civic elections will take place. Pompeii has already issued a list and wants us to persuade those on the list."

"Voting, which candidates for important positions are yet to be determined?"

At the luxurious Roman aristocratic banquet, Henry found himself completely surrounded by various Roman women, while Julius and Valerius Aurelius sat in the relatively sparse courtyard, discussing the upcoming work.

Since Julius and Valerius Aurelius had already sided with the Triumvirs, this year, those associated with the Triumvirs would start influencing the senators in the Senate. The core of all actions was to ensure that the candidates for next year's positions, such as the consuls and the tribunes of the plebs, were aligned with the Triumvirs.

"The plebeian tribune is almost certain, but we need to pay attention to the votes for the tribune of the treasury. Many nobles are not satisfied with the candidate proposed by Pompeii. So, we might have to personally visit each one and persuade them. Convince them to cast their votes for Artorius Gaius."

Valerius Aurelius first threw out the progress of the work and the challenges, then reclined in his chair, observing Julius's reaction. In fact, Julius, having recently joined the side of the Triumvirs, had Valerius Aurelius assigned to him by Pompeii to observe and take note of this declining Roman noble. If necessary, Valerius Aurelius could also send people to probe him. Julius was completely unaware of Valerius Aurelius's cunning and the hidden tasks behind. However, when faced with the question raised by his good friend, Julius quickly responded.

Chapter 10

"We'll set off tomorrow, acting separately. I'll go find each person on the list one by one. But there's one problem: what if we can't persuade them, or if these people suddenly change their minds on the day of the election? What do we do then?"

Julius had always regarded Valerius Aurelius as his sworn brother. Still, in the treacherous and scheming Roman aristocratic society, true friends were hard to find. Although Valerius Aurelius mostly considered Julius, his old companion, a genuine friend, after experiencing too much betrayal and conspiracy, Valerius Aurelius no longer dared to trust anyone completely. The nobles had too many deep layers of deceit, and beneath each layer unveiled, there were more conspiracies. Therefore, in Julius's question, Valerius Aurelius left a considerable amount of room, not revealing the entire plan.

"Persuading someone to do something typically involves two methods – money and intimidation. If, by then, someone refuses to follow your advice and vote for Artorius, you can easily resolve it with money. If that's not enough, you can come to me. Pompeii has already allocated a portion of the assets for me to handle, but you know, most of that money belongs to Crassus. As for dealing with those who can't be swayed even with money, I believe you know how to handle it. You have so many excellent assassins under you; I think many people will still comply when a sword is at their neck."

Valerius Aurelius said coldly. Julius even suspected that his friend of more than ten years, his comrade, was no longer as sincere and trusting as he used to be. His eyes were deep and profound, devoid of the trust and sincerity from his youth.

His methods were no longer straightforward but filled with cunning and treachery. But in the war for power, such was the way. Behind the seemingly quiet and peaceful Senate, a storm had long been brewing in secret.

"Alright, that's the plan. Tomorrow, let's tackle the list. Tonight, let's not dwell on heavy topics. Come on, let's go outside and immerse ourselves in the festive atmosphere."

Seeing Julius's worried expression, Valerius Aurelius changed the topic, injecting a new life into the mood. As Pompeii's trusted assistant, working for the Triumvirs, Valerius Aurelius could only say so much. The next steps depended on Julius's performance. Whether he could be trusted or not, or if the core figures of the Triumvirs had to intervene, everything remained uncertain. Until then, Valerius Aurelius had to maintain a certain level of caution and constant observation.

"I heard that during Caesar's arena matches, you commanded your men to defeat a legion formation of gladiators. Was that your slave?"

In the courtyard of a Roman mansion, the conversation among men differed from that of Roman noblewomen. The women mainly discussed entertainment and the pleasures of life. Thermal baths, strong gladiator slaves, silk, and spices were topics they enthusiastically talked about. A few Roman women might involve themselves in political matters, but the mother of a giant like Odavus was perhaps an exception. However, she hadn't appeared in Roman history yet.

Chapter 10

"Octavius, the slave you're talking about."

Agrippina didn't use a question mark but directly mentioned Henry's name. This gladiator slave "noble" Agrippina was quite familiar with. There wasn't a man she couldn't have except for Octavius, which was Henry's Roman name in this world. Each success achieved by Octavius was like a slap in the face, revealing her past misdeeds to her husband. Octavius, leveraging the arena, had become a sensational star, a gem in Julius's possession. Thus, trying to manipulate this boy again became increasingly impossible for her. When it came to Henry, Agrippina undoubtedly gritted her teeth.

"How about it? Has that slave come today? I'm sure you've brought him. Come on, let me see him."

Valiant gladiator, so charming, your (omit two hundred words). In any case, Roman gladiators were always idols admired by women. They were manly and valiant. Valerius Aurelius's wife was even eager to meet this legendary gladiator.

"Yes."

Reluctantly, Agrippina led other noblewomen to Henry. When the official's wives arrived, the * women tactfully retreated, allowing these upper-class noblewomen to interact with their idol.

"As a gladiator, he's not strong enough. Oh, I mean, he's not as tall as I imagined."

Livia did not participate in Caesar's gladiator matches, so she had not seen Henry's appearance. In the eyes of Romans, a gladiator with such achievements should be a robust man, even more robust than the Gauls. But Henry's first impression on Livia was that this gladiator was still a child. Nevertheless, he was undeniably charming.

Livia approached Henry again.

From this distance, Henry could once again smell the strong scent emanating from this Roman woman. Obviously, just like Bolivia, this woman from the Valerius Aurelius family lived a luxurious life. These women were not what Henry was looking for, but in the current environment, he had to adapt.

"He looks inexperienced."

After approaching and quickly leaving Henry, Livia's comment on his lack of experience carried a clear meaning that the other women present understood. They all revealed wicked smiles.

The cool moonlight shrouded the Roman noble mansion like a thin veil. In this hazy moonlight, people washed away the fatigue of the day and gathered for a party. Wheat from Sicily, olive oil grown in Rome, and grapes from the Gaul region – everything here reflected the extravagant desires of the Roman nobles.

"Are you the legendary gladiator who fought ten against one in the arena that day?"

Chapter 10

After Livia left, another Roman noblewoman walked up to Henry and stood in front of him. However, looking at this woman's appearance, she differed from all the other Roman noblewomen.

Firstly, she shouldn't be called a woman or a lady; calling her a young lady would be more appropriate. Her delicately small face needed no makeup, and her elegant and noble temperament had no hint of artificiality. The pure and beautiful girl suddenly appearing amidst the heavily made-up Roman noblewomen left Henry somewhat at a loss.

Judging by Henry's previous conversations with Roman noblewomen, he usually displayed a certain level of respect. However, that was only surface-level. In his heart, Henry disapproved of these debauched Roman noblewomen. Though this Roman girl belonged to the aristocracy, she exuded a fresh and refined aura. Perhaps she hadn't been tainted by the societal norms?

The girl asked politely, "Fighting ten opponents at once is just a rumor, and I dare not assume the title of a legend."

Henry stared at the girl for a good three seconds before snapping back to reality, answering humbly, "You're quite unique."

The girl spoke again, maintaining a distance from Henry, unlike other noblewomen who tended to get too close to the gladiator.

"Really?" Henry didn't know how to converse with this

somewhat different girl. Just like in his pre-transcendence days, an otaku always found himself at a loss in front of beautiful women, often blushing after a few words. Henry embraced this tradition, standing in front of the girl, unsure of how to initiate a conversation.

"Both of you, step aside. I want to talk to this gladiator alone."

The elegant noble girl dismissed the guards. Despite Henry being a star in the arena, he couldn't escape his slave status. Two Roman soldiers always kept a close watch on this beast, no matter the occasion.

Reluctant to leave, the guards hesitated for only two seconds. Then, the two Roman soldiers tactfully walked away, but Henry's hands remained in shackles.

"Come, let's sit over here and chat for a while."

Henry followed the Roman noble girl, appearing quite uncomfortable. Although the audience was small, the glances were filled with curiosity.

The girl led Henry to a garden balcony where few people were present. It offered a view of the beautiful scenery outside, overlooking half of Rome from the villa built on the hills.

Witnessing such a beautiful night scene for the first time, the introverted Henry suddenly felt an urge to burst into tears. The scenery, once only seen in movies before his transcendence, was now perfectly replicated here. Oh, not replicated but even

Chapter 10

more beautiful than the movie scenes. Rome, like a brilliant gem under the night sky, reflected the gentle night scene in the bright moonlight. The scene of countless lights set against the backdrop showcased the tranquility and elegance of the moment.

"Haven't you seen such a view before?"

The girl looked at Octavius in front of her, asking curiously. Henry turned his head, awkwardly responding, "Um."

"By the way, they say you're a Gaul, but I think you look more like a Roman. What were you before becoming a gladiator?"

The elegant girl first changed the topic. The atmosphere of the conversation subtly shifted. Perhaps this girl in front of him didn't view him as a slave at all? Henry was somewhat pleased, but on second thought, it was unlikely. The concept of master and slave was deeply ingrained in this world, and without the progress of time, changing such views would be difficult.

"Before becoming a gladiator, I seemed to be a blacksmith's child? Or maybe a fisherman, going out to sea for fishing and encountering a storm, saved by someone? Anyway, I don't remember much. It was a brutal injury that erased my memories before being rescued."

Henry answered with courtesy, not just in words but also in demeanor. If one were to overlook the heavy shackles, people might even forget his slave status.

"I'm curious how you developed such an elegant demeanor. I guess you were a Roman noble before your injury."

The girl continued, seemingly jubilant to have found a different type of gladiator for herself. In reality, Henry was aware of it. His current body had indeed belonged to a Roman noble named Gaius before transcendence. However, that name carried too much family conflict and hatred. Except for Henry himself, he wouldn't tell anyone. In this society filled with blood and treachery, having a bit more cunning was always advantageous.

"Being praised by you is my honor, madam."

Henry politely replied, and every elegant response and demeanor seemed to arouse a new curiosity and expectation in the Roman girl's eyes.

"Gladiator, do you know Greek history? Many Roman nobles are studying and learning from Greek classical culture, but I find those things flashy and impractical. However, my brother loves researching them."

The girl tried to engage Henry in more conversation, perhaps hoping that this gladiator, with his distinctive appearance and demeanor, would understand her words.

"Yes, Greek civilization is one of the brightest pages in human history. Its architecture, art, and philosophy are all worthy of praise and study by future generations. Especially the philosophical achievements, with three great philosophers—Socrates, Plato, and Aristotle."

Chapter 10

As Henry spoke these words, tears welled up in his eyes. It had been so long since he arrived in this ancient Roman society, and finally, someone could talk to him about things beyond eating, sleeping, and fighting. In the previous months at the gladiator slave school, although he got along well with his comrades, the crude gladiators couldn't discuss anything other than fighting and roaming. Tonight, the appearance of this Roman noble girl undoubtedly provided Henry with a good opportunity. At least, he had a listening companion.

"You actually know Aristotle?"

The girl's voice suddenly rose, seemingly unable to control her surprise.

"Yes, he is a famous philosopher in ancient Greek history, a student of Plato, and also a teacher of Alexander. He taught…"

Henry stood in front of the girl, speaking eloquently, oblivious to the utterly astonished expression on the Roman girl's face.

The moonlight of the night stretched the silhouettes of the two people. Although the girl's attendants were around, the two of them found a kindred spirit, extending the conversation to various topics—society, economy, and the lives of the people. They completely disregarded the feelings of those around them and the odd glances they received.

"You are the most polite and knowledgeable gladiator I've ever met. It's a pity for someone like you to fight in the arena with those slaves."

"But I am still a slave, a gladiator. Where else can I go besides the arena?"

In the end, Henry had to bring his thoughts back to reality. Despite knowing so much about this era, it was all in his mind. Without a suitable position, even if you had extensive knowledge, there was no place to apply it. However, the only gain tonight was that he had at least met a beautiful and refined girl. Although he didn't know her name and wasn't sure if they would meet again.

"Perhaps I should introduce you to my brother; he loves knowledge of Greek literature and philosophy."

The girl said as she was about to get up. At this moment, the nighttime banquet was coming to an end.

"Your brother? What is his name?"

As soon as the words were spoken, Henry felt he might have been a bit too incautious. An enslaved person and a noble were entirely different groups, and such questions could only arise among nobility. The attendants quickly shot angry glares and seemed motivated to inflict punishment on Henry. However, the girl promptly stopped them and casually answered, "My brother's name is Octavius Turinus."

The girl left the balcony under the escort of her attendants, leaving Henry standing there, stunned for a long time, like an ancient Roman statue, petrified... Octavius, Augustus, the sole legal heir to Caesar, the future creator of the Roman Empire's

Chapter 10

imperial system. Despite being only a 15-year-old child at the moment.

Chapter 11

The night descended, and within the Gladius Magnus Ludus Gladiator School, as the moon concealed itself behind dark clouds, the training sessions came to an end. Gladiators returned to their quarters in pairs, leaving the training ground with only scattered torches flickering in the dim light. This enchanting night seemed to echo the scene of Henry meeting Agrippina on the villa balcony, though lacking the presence of that intoxicating girl, leaving Henry feeling a bit lonely.

He turned and looked at his Numidian companion, Septimus, asking suddenly, "Septimus, do you still miss your wife?"

Septimus clearly didn't expect Henry to ask such a question, but he quickly understood his friend's thoughts.

"Brother, are you thinking about a woman?" Septimus asked

Chapter 11

with a teasing tone, injecting a hint of playfulness into the previously serious atmosphere.

"No, no," Henry denied with a smile, a happy expression unconsciously appearing on his face. It had been half a year since he arrived in this ancient Roman world, and never before had he longed for a girl as he did now. Agrippina's graceful figure and delicate face kept appearing in his mind, like a dream but so vividly real.

"Don't try to fool me, brother. I've seen many women. Tell me, which girl are you missing? I'll talk to her for you." Septimus continued to tease, and the Gladiator King falling in love became big news at the Gladius Magnus Ludus school. Who could this noble girl be that had captivated the genius gladiator's heart?

"You can't help me," Henry turned to Septimus, looking at him. This Numidian, with his radiant face, always seemed to maintain an optimistic attitude.

"Why?" Septimus persistently inquired, his face still carrying a childlike innocence. On the arena, Septimus and Henry were like two bloodthirsty beasts, but at this moment, they were like two innocent children, playfully bantering with each other.

"Because the woman I love is Agrippina, the sister of Gaius Octavius Turinus." When Henry said these words, he noticed Septimus's previously playful expression instantly turning serious. Septimus didn't know who Gaius Octavius was, but the surname Gaius held a lofty status in Roman society. Septimus understood that Henry was in love not with an ordinary noblewoman but with someone from the Gaius family. His friend, his comrade, was in love with a noblewoman, and that would only bring him misfortune, not happiness and fulfillment.

"Henry, Octavius, brother, you know, for more than half a year, I've considered you my closest friend, the most loyal comrade. We fought side by side, bled together. For the sake of our brotherly bond, I advise you to sever this thought early. Noble women are not what we should be yearning for, especially from the Gaius family. I don't know exactly what kind of nobility they are, but they surely possess power and prestige. You cannot be with her. Moreover, if your relationship is discovered, you'll face life-threatening danger. Remember, nobles can order the killing of slaves with just a word. Slaves can only marry slaves; that's Roman law."

Septimus stared at Henry, expressing his concerns and opinions when no one was around. However, Henry had long known everything Septimus said, but he couldn't control his emotions. Confronted daily with those debauched and frivolous Roman prostitutes, he suddenly encountered a pure and elegant girl, and Henry felt helpless to resist.

"I know everything you're saying, but maybe there's another way?" Henry asked persistently.

"Stop dreaming, brother. My wife is just a wall away, yet she's married to someone else. Are you hoping that the noblewoman will wait for you to gain freedom, become a knight, and

Chapter 11

eventually marry you? Brother, we must face reality. The reality is that we are gladiators, slaves, people without freedom."

Septimus's realistic words shattered Henry's ideals in an instant, but he still came with the knowledge of a time traveler. Perhaps one day, he could achieve something great? In that case, everything was possible. However, forming an attachment to someone might take only three seconds, but forgetting required much more time. Henry realized he was a bit naive, but he couldn't let go of this connection in his heart.

In the mansion of the Valerius Aurelius family, a conspiracy was brewing.

"Valerius Aurelius, did you notice what happened at the banquet the day before yesterday?" Livia addressed her husband.

If the life and thoughts of Roman commoners were simple and superficial, the hearts of the nobility were filled with conspiracies and schemes. Even the tiniest details could become their leverage and tools for stirring up trouble and making a big fuss.

Agrippina's performance at the Julius banquet caught Livia's attention. Despite the many attendees and a plethora of dramatic performances that day, Livia keenly observed Agrippina's special fondness for that gladiator.

No one knew what they discussed on the rooftop. Livia merely watched from a distance, but judging from the innocent girl's expression, it wasn't disdain or mockery towards a slave. It was a strong curiosity and interest in the unknown.

"That gladiator?" Valerius Aurelius replied from the luxurious bed, half-reclining. He didn't understand why his wife suddenly brought up the gathering from two days ago or what purpose or discovery lay behind it. As a man, he only saw this: a strong gladiator surrounded by a group of Roman women, a scene as ordinary as it could be. If Livia was indeed referring to that incident, Valerius Aurelius couldn't summon much interest.

"No, the noble girl who was talking to that gladiator," Livia sat at the edge of the bed, trying to remind her husband of what he should pay attention to.

"Who is she?" Valerius Aurelius turned his gaze to Livia, hoping she wouldn't beat around the bush.

"Agrippina."

"You mean Domitia's daughter?" Valerius Aurelius quickly caught on. Priscilla, as Caesar's niece, pleasing her meant expressing support for Caesar. (At this time, Caesar had already been appointed governor of the northern three provinces, commanding six legions, and achieving initial success in Gaul. Following Caesar promised a bright future.) Of course, the gift had to be given secretly, without letting Pompeii know. It was best to make the outside world believe that Julius was sending gifts to Priscilla, expressing his desire to join Caesar, not Valerius Aurelius himself, especially since Valerius Aurelius was currently working under Pompeii. Although the three-headed alliance maintained a unified front, there were still some minor

Chapter 11

conflicts between the three heads, especially between Caesar and Pompeii. Utilizing Octavius, the gladiator, to give gifts to Priscilla not only signaled to Caesar that he was on his side but also allowed Pompeii to direct his dissatisfaction towards Julius. After the team battle in the arena, everyone knew that Octavius belonged to Julius.

On the surface, this seemed beneficial to Valerius Aurelius without harming him. However, it entailed scheming against his good friend Julius. Nevertheless, after so many years in the Senate's twists and turns, Valerius Aurelius no longer held the so-called brotherly bonds in such high regard. Everything centered around interests to stand firmly in the complex upper echelons of Roman society and continuously climb the peaks of power.

"This sounds like a good suggestion. My wife, Livia, your keen perception has helped me once again. How should I thank Venus (the Roman goddess of love) for the gift she has bestowed upon me?" Valerius Aurelius said happily, embracing his wife. Yet, in this seemingly sweet embrace, Livia also knew that there wasn't much of the past affection between her and this man. As time's passage stripped away the once fiery passion and desire, the sweetness now was more built on the mutual pursuit of power. If today, Livia couldn't help Valerius Aurelius achieve his ambitions, perhaps, at this moment by his side, was already another woman he could use.

Chapter 12

When Valerius Aurelius brought Henry to Gaius Octavius's house, Agrippina excitedly ran out of the room. She had been worried about finding a legitimate reason to introduce Octavius to her brother, and now, Valerius Aurelius had unexpectedly delivered this gladiator right to her doorstep.

Watching Agrippina's enthusiastic expression, Henry couldn't help but feel an unusual joy. However, as he surveyed the surroundings and noticed Priscilla's expression and the cunning look on Valerius Aurelius's face, Henry had a vague sense of something.

Gift-giving among the nobility often carried special motives and intentions. Why would they choose him as a gift for Priscilla instead of any other gladiator? Could it be that Valerius Aurelius sensed something during their time at the villa in the

Chapter 12

mountains with Agrippina? Otherwise, this not particularly wealthy noble wouldn't have purchased him at a high price from Julius, only to send him to Priscilla.

Henry's initial reaction was that he was once again being used, presented as a gift, a pawn in the struggle for power. Agrippina, still a naive girl, might think Valerius Aurelius was simply trying to please her parents out of goodwill.

"Priscilla, ah, it's been a long time since I last saw you. In these few months, you seem even more radiant and elegant than before."

Valerius Aurelius began showering Priscilla with lavish compliments upon seeing her. As Gaius Octavius had passed away, Priscilla met with visiting guests alone. Henry noticed that this Roman noblewoman, not particularly famous in history, possessed a noble and elegant demeanor, displaying a low-key and steady character. At first glance, she didn't seem like someone frivolous or shallow, a far cry from the Priscilla portrayed in television dramas.

"Thank you for your praise, Valerius Aurelius."

Priscilla glanced at the gladiator sent over, said nothing, and continued to treat the guests with fruits and milk. While Valerius Aurelius had also lived in Rome for an extended period, many times it wasn't convenient for him to move around. Despite the apparent calm in the Roman Senate, dangers lurked behind the scenes. A single misstep could land him in someone else's trap, making him a sacrificial pawn in the power struggle.

"Priscilla, today I brought a gift for you."

Meetings and discussions between nobles, especially before gift-giving, often involved some small talk and greetings. Valerius Aurelius was not surprised. However, after a long string of pleasantries, they needed to get to the point. This was Valerius Aurelius's purpose in coming here.

Walking behind Henry, Valerius Aurelius pressed his hand on the gladiator's shoulder, causing Henry discomfort. He felt like a commodity being sold, a tool in someone else's scheming. The female slaves in Priscilla's house gazed at him eagerly, like predators eyeing their prey. Agrippina, even though Henry wished to steal more glances at her, dared not show any signs. In the current situation, Caesar's niece, Priscilla, proved to be a formidable character. Although she remained composed, her thoughts were undoubtedly clear. Henry speculated that Gaius Octavius's success at a young age had much to do with his mother, Priscilla.

"Gladiator?"

Priscilla approached, her face still calm, as if she knew nothing and understood everything.

"Yes, he is the reigning champion of the Roman arena. Although he hasn't achieved a hundred victories yet, his performances in the arena are absolutely spectacular."

Valerius Aurelius spoke with a confident smile, enthusiastically narrating, and Agrippina also revealed excitement and antic-

Chapter 12

ipation. However, Priscilla maintained her calm expression throughout Valerius Aurelius's introduction.

In this villa, Henry continuously searched for the figure of the young Gaius Octavius, Agrippina's brother who loved books. However, the young Gaius Octavius never appeared; he was nowhere to be found.

"But our villa is too small, and unfortunately, we can't accommodate more gladiators. Besides, Agrippina and Gaius Octavius aren't fond of watching gladiator fights. So, thank you for your kindness, Valerius Aurelius, but you better take this skilled gladiator back with you."

"No, Mother, I enjoy watching gladiator fights."

Before Priscilla could finish her sentence, Agrippina hurriedly interjected. However, the next moment, Henry saw the stern expression and unquestionable authority of Priscilla as a mother.

Priscilla quickly used her gaze to stop Agrippina's naive and unwise behavior, and Agrippina saw her mother's stern and angry expression. Soon, Agrippina fell silent. Valerius Aurelius was left in an awkward situation.

Henry looked at Agrippina, feeling a sense of reluctance and helplessness. Everything here was not under his control. His fate was manipulated by cunning and deceitful nobles like Valerius Aurelius and Julius. As a slave, he had no chance to change his destiny. Achieving a hundred victories in the arena was just a means for the nobles to suppress slave uprisings. In history, how many gladiators had gained freedom through their efforts? Very few.

With these thoughts, Henry couldn't help but feel sorrowful.

"Valerius Aurelius, thank you for your kindness, but Gaius Octavius's villa is already filled with slaves from various places. So, you better take this robust gladiator back to your academy. He will have more opportunities and space to showcase his skills there."

At this moment, Henry finally saw the wise Priscilla looking at him, her gaze filled with appreciation. In this delicate situation, Priscilla had to make the most sensible choice and not get involved in any power struggles. Roman nobles, especially the elders in the Senate, wouldn't give you gifts for no reason. Priscilla was well aware of what lay hidden behind this.

"But..."

Valerius Aurelius wanted to say more, but Livia pulled on his garment from behind. Priscilla couldn't see this subtle movement, but she could feel that Valerius Aurelius's wife, standing behind him, was smarter and knew how to act according to the situation.

"Alright, Priscilla, I'll take this skillful gladiator back."

Valerius Aurelius called the guards to take Henry out of the villa, preparing to stuff him into a carriage. In the last glance, Henry

Chapter 12

looked at Agrippina in front of him, filled with reluctance. But under the escort of the guards, he had to leave this beautiful mansion.

Perhaps due to the disruption of the gift-giving plan, Valerius Aurelius temporarily forgot to instruct the guards. When Henry was being put into the carriage, he wasn't blindfolded or dressed. Instead, he stood at the doorstep of Gaius Octavius's house, allowing passersby to cast curious glances at the scene. The champion gladiator from the Julius family had ended up at the doorstep of Gaius Octavius's house? What was Julius planning to do?

Henry believed that everyone passing by had such thoughts, but they dared not speak them out loud.

How long Valerius Aurelius and Priscilla chatted before coming out, Henry didn't know. He only saw that when this cunning noble couple walked out of Gaius Octavius's house, they were covered in high cloaks, making it almost impossible for onlookers to see their faces…

With a sense of grievance and confusion, Agrippina questioned her mother's recent decision.

"The era of the Roman Republic has passed. What we see in Rome now, although it still has institutions like the Senate, is no longer the same Senate as before. Since your uncle Caesar, together with Pompey and Crassus, formed the Triumvirate, the actual power in Rome is in their hands. However, just like the Senate, there are conflicts within the Triumvirate. Despite the apparent harmony, Pompey has opinions about Caesar because Caesar's achievements and reputation are gradually surpassing his."

Priscilla, a shrewd woman, faced her daughter's innocence today. She initially didn't want to reveal these intricacies, but fearing Agrippina's future mischief, Priscilla decided to tell her daughter the truth.

"But how does that relate to us accepting Octavius?"

Agrippina continued to inquire, her beautiful face revealing innocence, like an inexperienced young girl. In reality, she was indeed too naive at the age of seventeen. She was not only insensitive to political affairs but also lacked the basic judgment of people.

"Valerius Aurelius wouldn't just give us a talented gladiator for no reason. The price of that slave is not a small number, especially now that he's famous. Accepting such a generous gift will undoubtedly attract attention. Even if Valerius Aurelius hides it well, over time, when others visit our villa, they will see that gladiator. Then, those cunning politicians will know that we accepted a gift from Valerius Aurelius or Julius. This news would make Pompey think that more Romans are leaning towards Caesar rather than him. The not-so-solid Triumvirate would become more tense due to various suspicions."

Priscilla took a sip of milk and continued.

"Currently, during Caesar's sensitive campaign in Gaul, Pom-

Chapter 12

pey is already dissatisfied with Caesar's achievements. If he learns that more Roman nobles, knights, and even Senate officials are siding with Caesar, it would undoubtedly make Pompey think differently. This wouldn't be favorable for Caesar. Now, Caesar is fighting in Gaul, his army is not yet formed, and Gaul is not yet conquered. If there is unrest within Rome at this time, it would be detrimental to Caesar. So, the more sensitive the situation, the more we cannot entertain any gestures of goodwill from Roman Senators, knights, or officials. Octa, my daughter, can you understand a bit?"

In the quiet Gaius mansion, after Priscilla quietly explained these cause-and-effect relationships, only seventeen-year-old Agrippina seemed unable to accept it. As an underage girl, hearing such complex interpersonal relationships for the first time, she felt sorrow for her own background. The young girl only wanted a peaceful life, to grow old with her beloved, but now it seemed that her future years would be spent in this endless struggle for power.

For the first time, Agrippina, the young girl, empathized with her mother. As Caesar's niece, a relative, how had she endured these years in such a cruel and treacherous environment?

"Mother, even so, do you still have to send my brother to Caesar's side?"

The young Agrippina's eyes were teary. Regardless of whether it was her mother or her dear brother Gaius Octavius, she had deep feelings for both. She didn't want to see the people closest to her entangled in this dark and desperate power struggle.

"Agrippina, my daughter, you must accept reality. Gaius Octavius has traits different from ordinary people. He is a sharp eagle. Although he is still young, he possesses a natural and keen insight into human affairs and the treacherous nature of people. For him, these seemingly complex and dangerous interpersonal relationships are a kind of enjoyment. When I teach him these things, he even enjoys pondering them with his own mind, and he doesn't feel tired. Perhaps your brother Gaius Octavius is naturally a politician, chosen by the Roman gods. One day, he may become the ruler of the Roman Republic. If that's the case, we cannot go against the will of Jupiter."

Sobs...

Priscilla finished explaining, and young Agrippina couldn't control her emotions, letting tears flow freely, soaking her clothes. She seemed to see the future years, trapped in that luxurious Roman villa. Like an injured kitten locked inside, she indulged in Rome's most luxurious wealth, yet felt an overwhelming emptiness inside. Her mother Priscilla and her still-young brother Gaius Octavius were both elites of this era in Rome. Perhaps the gods had chosen them, burdening them with too much responsibility.

In the Roman noble villa in the mountains:

"Livia, I never expected Priscilla to be such a cunning and profound woman. She's a sly fox, always hiding and masquerading in the shadows. We all overlooked her, but her scheming may surpass all of us. I shouldn't have underestimated her. Damn."

Chapter 12

Returning from Gaius Octavius's mansion, Valerius Aurelius angrily rebuked. However, the esteemed Roman noble seemed to have not foreseen the severity of the problem. It wasn't until Valerius Aurelius's wife Livia reminded him again:

"Now is not the time to discuss this trivial matter, my husband, Valerius Aurelius. Have you noticed the way the Roman citizens looked at Octavius when we left Priscilla's house?"

If Valerius Aurelius was a bold and daring wolf, then Livia was the venomous snake standing behind this wolf. Every time Valerius Aurelius fell short, Livia could timely remind him and guide him to use more ruthless methods. This time, Livia's reminder once again made Valerius Aurelius notice this detail.

Having Octavius (Henry) wait for him at Gaius Octavius's house door was initially just a secondary plan after the success of the gift-giving. But now, Priscilla hadn't accepted his gift, and Octavius was seen by passersby, possibly even by Pompey's informants and trusted ones.

The purchase of Octavius was known only to Valerius Aurelius and Julius's families. More Roman citizens were unaware of this, and even Pompey and the Senate were in the dark. After all, trading slaves was commonplace, and who would bother to pay attention? However, that was precisely the problem.

Now, Octavius appeared at the gate of Gaius Octavius's house, seen by Roman citizens and possibly Pompey's spies. If this information reached Pompey, considering his current distrust and dissatisfaction with Caesar, he would likely believe that

Julius had betrayed him, sided with Valerius Aurelius, and then switched to Caesar's side. In that case, Pompey would undoubtedly take action against Julius. Furthermore, if Julius learned about this, knowing that Valerius Aurelius bought Octavius as a gift for Priscilla, what would Julius think? Would he believe that Valerius Aurelius intentionally set a trap for him?

All of this Valerius Aurelius didn't consider when he left Priscilla's house. Now, his wife Livia had to remind him once again. Although it was a small detail, it could lead to an unfortunate outcome. So, now, Valerius Aurelius had to reconsider his plans.

Chapter 13

On a summer night, the gentle breeze caressed Henry's face as he stood in the alley under the eaves, gazing at the crowds bustling on the nearby noble avenue. He felt like the whole world had come alive.

The life of a slave gladiator was far from that of a commoner. Most of the time, Henry was confined to the underground dungeons of some noble mansion or the cells of the gladiator school. He seldom had the opportunity to venture outside. Despite spending half a year in this ancient Roman world, Henry rarely had the chance to experience the vibrancy and grandeur of the millennium-old city.

However, Rome wasn't the luxurious spectacle Henry had imagined. More often than not, the entire city resembled a large pigsty, chaotic and disordered. Streets and alleys were like a dense spider web, with civilians and animals sharing the same living space in the populous districts, muddy paths winding through. Everywhere, various storefronts cluttered the already narrow roads.

The walls of the dilapidated apartments were covered in vulgar and mundane graffiti. The noisy crowd roamed freely through the disorderly streets. Small vendors and peddlers dominated the scene, and sometimes, one could witness disputes between clients and madams over pricing in the alleys.

Henry roamed around the Roman noble mansion, cloaked in secrecy, preventing anyone from getting a clear look at him. From dusk until dark, the crowded and noisy crowd gradually subsided as people returned to their homes to prepare their dinners.

The dense housing apartments were stacked side by side, mostly brick and wood structures. In case of a fire, it would quickly spread as a chain reaction. Witnessing this scene, Henry easily understood the path to wealth taken by that shrewd businessman Crassus. It was said that upon seeing the chaotic sight of Rome, Crassus founded the only professional firefighting squad at the time. They rushed to any place with a fire, but extinguishing fires wasn't an obligation; it came at a price.

Moreover, during the spread of a large fire, this cunning businessman intentionally delayed the process. This compelled the commoners to sell their houses to him at the cheapest price to avoid their homes being consumed by the flames. After extinguishing the fire, Crassus would then rent out the

Chapter 13

properties at exorbitant prices, amassing considerable wealth through these despicable means.

Thinking about this, Henry couldn't help but feel a wave of sorrow for Rome in this era. Gaius Octavius was right – "I found Rome a city of bricks and left it a city of marble." If we evaluate contributions to Rome, Henry even thought that Gaius Octavius surpassed Caesar. However, the present Gaius Octavius should still be an eleven or twelve-year-old child.

Two assassins followed behind Henry, not knowing what the champion gladiator was thinking. They continued to trail him around Dubnillus's mansion, thinking he was merely studying the surroundings for a potential escape later.

In the end, Henry chose to stop at a corner of a small alley. This location was closest to the main entrance of Dubnillus's mansion. If Valerius Aurelius was right, the great noble would come out from this exit soon to attend a private banquet.

Actually, this was a conspiracy itself. Regardless of whether he succeeded in the next step, Henry knew he had long been used by these noble elders, and there wasn't a good outcome awaiting him. Valerius Aurelius wouldn't be genuinely kind, doing the job for him and then granting freedom. Dubnillus might not be easy to deal with either; influential nobles like him wouldn't lack guards. The assassination mission might be a charade itself, but Henry had no freedom of choice.

The mansion's gate slowly creaked open, and the noble, draped in luxurious evening robes, walked out, followed by two guards.

Then this somewhat portly man only embraced his wife after a while.

"Move."

Under the cover of night, Henry gestured to the two companions behind him, and they silently moved forward together.

The assassination mission couldn't take place right at Dubnillus's doorstep because the guards were inside the mansion. Striking too soon would swiftly attract a pursuit from numerous guards. However, time couldn't be dragged too long either. As Dubnillus approached the venue of the banquet, the crowd would increase, and the guards would tighten their vigilance.

So, it began with tracking, followed by finding a deserted street, and then swiftly taking care of business.

Two assassins accompanied Henry, lowering their cloaks and casually walking, trying not to draw much attention. On the bustling Phaes Avenue, pedestrians were still relatively abundant. Henry's movements didn't raise much notice from the guards. At most, they received an extra glance and then followed the lady of the house into the mansion. As the gates closed, the assassination operation officially commenced.

Amid the hazy lamplights, the figure of the noble stretched long under the moonlight. Two guards fully armed accompanied Dubnillus closely.

Three young individuals, draped in thick cloaks, silently

Chapter 13

approached the unfortunate noble in the night.

"Halt!"

The guards instinctively turned around, but it was too late. The two assassins swiftly struck, their razor-sharp daggers going from hand to throat in the blink of an eye. One hand tightly covered the mouth of the victim as the guards struggled fiercely, losing their last breath in the brutal struggle.

The pitiful noble, witnessing the bloody scene, retreated while crawling and shouting in panic, "What do you want? I'll give you anything, money, right? I have plenty. You can come with me, and I'll get it for you."

Perhaps nobles were all so terrified of death before facing it? Henry wanted to spare this plump noble a moment of mercy, but unfortunately, he was now a slave and had to follow his master's orders. Otherwise, returning would be a dead-end for him. Moreover, there was no place to escape; his slave mark made him easily identifiable by every Roman guard.

"I'm sorry, Lord Dubnillus."

Henry approached, grabbing the collar of the fallen wealthy noble. The dagger glinted with a chilling light under the moon. The sudden bloody scene caused several pedestrians passing by to scream and dodge.

"I'm not Dubnillus. You've got the wrong person."

Not Dubnillus?

In an instant, all the previous doubts and speculations were confirmed...

Henry reluctantly let go of the trembling unfortunate soul on the ground. The next moment, dozens of fully armed Roman guards surged out from the alleys on both sides of the street.

"This is a conspiracy!"

The two assassins who came with Henry shouted.

However, there was no chance for explanations.

Staring at the magnificent palace on the hill, shimmering with red light not far away, Henry couldn't help but sigh. Those nobles and senators luxuriating in their palaces and mansions today, how many innocent lives did they step on to climb up? Behind their extravagant desires, how many people had to sacrifice and bear the burden?

Henry chose not to kill the obese middle-aged noble but let him go. Even as the guards rushed up, encircling him, his two companions wanted to resist desperately, but Henry had already given up resistance. Dozens of Roman guards, armed with javelins and short swords, surrounded them. If these "criminals" tried to escape, dozens of long spears would be thrown, and even if Achilles himself possessed them, escape would be impossible.

Chapter 13

Henry dropped his weapons, and the leader of the Roman city patrol squad, wearing a sly smile, produced the prepared handcuffs…

Chapter 14

"Octavius, the once-renowned gladiator in the Roman arena, is now completely unrelated to the Julius family. The ruthless Julius sold this gladiator king at a high price to a senator of the Roman Senate, Valerius Aurelius, a week ago."

In the bustling Roman market, a bald Greek freeman stood on a platform, loudly announcing the document drafted by Julius, informing the citizens of Rome that the legendary gladiator, who rose to fame overnight, had no connection with him. In the peak of his gladiator career, he had been sold at the best price to someone else.

However, the crowd remained unconvinced. In Roman history, there had never been a slave owner or noble merchant who sold their gladiator, especially right when they gained fame. Even a fool knew that the initial period when a champion

Chapter 14

gladiator emerged was the most lucrative for the slave owner. At that time, the appearance fee and the prize money for each victorious match were at their peak. Selling a gladiator at this point, as Julius did, seemed equivalent to giving away a money-making machine.

Yet Julius couldn't reveal the real reasons to these unfortunate commoners. The struggle between the Senate and the Triumvirs was far beyond the knowledge of these underground citizens.

Just at this moment, a terrifying piece of news emanated from the nearby Roman judicial office – last night, the prominent noble Lucius had been assassinated, and the murderer, Octavius, the gladiator mentioned in Julius's documents, had been brought to justice.

The marketplace erupted into commotion as people rushed to hear this explosive news, paying little attention to the Greek man on the podium reading some sales contract. Considering Julius's behavior, many concluded that he fabricated this slave transaction proof to exonerate himself.

"Cursed! Cursed! Cursed!"

As the news reached Julius's home, he jumped up from his lunch, incessantly cursing the despicable Valerius Aurelius. Just yesterday, he had trusted Valerius so much, only to find out that, in order to climb the ladder with Caesar, Valerius had ruthlessly targeted him, using him as a shield, a sacrificial piece in his plan.

While the servants were conveying the news, the Roman city magistrate led a fully armed troop of guards into Julius's home.

The slaves busy with household chores fearfully made way for the guards. Such incidents were unheard of since their arrival at this place. Julius, though from a declining noble family, had been honest and low-key in the first half of his life, never imagining that such a day would come.

Everything was just a sacrifice in the power struggle. Julius finally realized, but there was no defense left. Perhaps, from the moment he placed trust in Valerius Aurelius, he sowed the seeds of endless suffering for himself.

Bolivia watched in terror as several Roman guards, like brutes, hauled her husband, who was changing clothes, and callously marched out of the courtyard. The guards paid no attention to Bolivia, as her father, Quintus Marcellus, was a wealthy man in Rome, akin to Crassus, working as a tax collector and secretly supporting the Triumvirs. Hence, the guards didn't arrest this panicked mistress, merely passing by her as if she were invisible.

In the courtyard, Julius's body was roughly dragged away. Passing by the edge of the water basin, the splashing water drops showered this unfortunate nobleman.

In just one day, so much had happened. Julius sent his steward to deliver documents to the Roman public officials who were reading news, then came the sensational news of Lucius's assassination spreading through the streets of Rome, and now,

Chapter 14

the city magistrate was swaggering into his home. Julius connected all the events and realized that everything had been premeditated.

"Mark Octavius, you are accused of murdering the prominent noble Lucius. Now, tell everyone, who instructed you to commit this heinous act?"

The day Julius was arrested, Henry was brought to the judicial hall by the guards, where curious nobles and officials had gathered. Such a terrorizing murder case in the capital of the Republic intrigued everyone, and they wanted to know who was behind it. However, Octavius was a slave of the Julius family, a fact well-known to everyone. They were more interested in understanding Julius's motive for murdering Lucius.

"..."

Facing the baseless accusations of the magistrate, Henry initially thought of defending the innocent Julius, but the words lingered on his lips. This was a conspiracy from the beginning. Valerius Aurelius sent him to assassinate a prominent Roman named Dubnillus, but he directed the blame toward another ordinary Roman noble. There was deception involved, and everything was premeditated by Valerius Aurelius, including the framing of Julius and Henry's capture. Faced with such a meticulously planned conspiracy, what could he possibly defend?

With that realization, Henry fell silent.

However, the magistrate signaled to the guards, and one of them, like a ruthless executioner, delivered a powerful punch to Henry's face. In the intense pain, Henry felt as if his nasal bone was about to crack open. Crimson blood began to spurt from his mouth and nostrils. This massive guard seemed specialized in such brutal tasks, threatening and coercing confessions from so-called criminals.

"It was Julius. He ordered me to assassinate that wealthy noble."

Facing the ferocious guard and the gloating spectators, Henry, in helplessness, made a mournful statement, shifting all the blame onto his original master—Julius. This was precisely what Valerius Aurelius and the magistrate wanted to hear.

After uttering these words, the magistrate immediately revealed a satisfied smile.

How much had Valerius Aurelius bribed this man? Why was he so diligently working for him? Henry looked at the chief magistrate, feeling that the Roman nobility before him was simply repugnant. In such a dark and corrupt society, where was justice to be found? Yet, he was still a slave—what else could he do? To survive was the best answer he could give to himself.

"So, what drove Julius to commit such a heinous act, to assassinate an unarmed Roman merchant?" The magistrate continued to inquire. This was the motive that the nobles and merchants present needed to know.

Chapter 14

Asking a slave to reveal his master's motives? How absurd that sounded. Yet, the magistrate proceeded with such a question, perhaps not even requiring evidence but just seeking the testimony he wanted from Henry. Despite the ludicrous and laughable nature of this testimony, who cared? All that mattered was the outcome.

"Because that Roman merchant once deceived Julius in a large-scale business deal. He adulterated the grain with yellow sand, mixing it into the cargo unnoticed. Only when Julius's men opened the grain boxes, inspecting them one by one, did they discover that sixty percent of the grain was adulterated with yellow sand and fine soil. However, Julius had already paid for the goods. When he confronted the merchant, he denied any wrongdoing. This deal caused Julius a significant financial loss, so he harbored resentment and devised this insane assassination plan."

As Henry's words fell, the venue erupted into a buzz. Everyone exchanged glances, shocked that a Roman of legitimate nobility like Julius could stoop to such a despicable act. While everyone outwardly displayed a surprised expression, deep down, they all knew how absurd it was for a slave to be aware of his master's plans and business matters. It was a ridiculous testimony. Yet, no one dared to object because witnesses and evidence were all present—undeniably present.

Henry's statement pleased the magistrate even more. Clearly, without prior notice, this gladiator slave could still cooperate so cleverly. The magistrate even entertained the idea of lenient treatment for Henry.

"Valerius Aurelius, why did you scheme against Octavius and collude with Roman nobles? I know the undeniable truth behind this story. Just two days ago, you delivered Octavius to our house, making him his new master. Yet, you instructed him to assassinate Lucius, an act unrelated to you. Then, you framed Julius. Why did you act this way?!"

The next day, Henry was thrown into prison, and news of this crime spread widely in Rome, reaching the ears of Gaius Octavius. Agrippina, learning of this news, hurriedly made her way to Valerius Aurelius's mansion. She didn't mince words with this cunning Roman noble.

"Young Agrippina, some things are not as simple as you think. What you see and hear may not necessarily be true. Come in, and let's discuss how we should proceed next. I also intend to rescue my gladiator."

Valerius Aurelius, upon seeing Agrippina, wasn't surprised. He promptly invited the young girl inside. The outside world was tumultuous, and Valerius Aurelius feared another complication.

"Explain the reasons and consequences of all this."

Agrippina threw off her cloak, glaring at the wily Roman noble with unabated anger. Valerius Aurelius found Agrippina's demeanor somewhat amusing. The young girl, still untouched by worldly hardships, might need years of experience to exhibit the same calmness as her mother. Valerius Aurelius smiled, not directly answering Agrippina's question but instead asking:

Chapter 14

"Does your mother know you're here?"

"No, I left her quietly."

Agrippina disdainfully replied, maintaining her sharp gaze on Valerius Aurelius. She had come to confront this Roman noble, also of aristocratic descent, hiding it from her mother for the sake of a gladiator. At times, Agrippina herself didn't understand what she was doing. Ever since that night in the mountain villa when she saw Octavius, she had been captivated by his noble aura, elegant speech, profound knowledge, and handsome appearance. He was like a precious piece of art that deeply moved the young girl's heart.

"Oh, I see. Well, since that's the case, we don't need to disturb your mother. I will find a way to rescue Octavius. Three days later, you go to the deepest part of the Rodris prison. I'll free Octavius, and then it's your responsibility to take him out of Rome. In Lucius's assassination case, I am also innocent."

"But..."

Agrippina wanted to say more, but Valerius Aurelius directly stopped her: "Now, immediately go back. When your mother Priscilla learns of this, she won't let it go so easily. By then, with investigations and tracking, Octavius won't escape the prison, and you won't see him again. Good girl, be obedient, go back now, and don't tell your mother you came to me."

Valerius Aurelius cajoled Agrippina while urging her to leave until she boarded her carriage. Only then did he reveal a cunning smile.

"Are you really planning to release that slave?"

After Agrippina left, Livia came out."Yes, Julius is beyond redemption, guilty as charged. Even if Cicero had a thousand defenses, they couldn't absolve him. Tomorrow, he'll be executed. As for Octavius, what can a slave do? Besides, in the court, he has already pointed out Julius's crimes. It seems he understands that he was manipulated, eager to please us, thinking that only by following me can he save his life. So, releasing him after Julius's execution poses no threat. At the same time, it can be considered a favor to Agrippina. Romans find it hard to refuse favors, isn't that right, my beautiful and intelligent wife?"

Valerius Aurelius explained confidently, for matters like these were inconsequential to a noble well-versed in political intrigue. Moreover, the crucial point was that he had done Agrippina a favor. In the future, if he needed the assistance of this young woman, today's favor would serve as an excellent pretext.

"Women are always easily lost in emotions, aren't they?"

Valerius Aurelius smiled, as if everything was proceeding perfectly.

"So, how do you plan to handle this? Octavius's execution is scheduled for five days from now."

As Valerius Aurelius finished speaking, Livia still felt a lingering

Chapter 14

unease. After all, Octavius was already a well-known figure in Rome. If he were discovered during his escape and pursued by the city guards, Valerius Aurelius might find himself in trouble.

"I will find a slave who resembles him, cover him in mud, mess up his hair, and then send him to the execution site in Octavius's place. The execution scene for Octavius only allows for a few hundred spectators, and not everyone will recognize that gladiator. Even if someone does, there's no evidence. Everything will be settled at the execution site."

Valerius Aurelius continued. His expression remained confident, for handling such matters was nothing significant for a noble well-versed in political intrigue. Moreover, there was Agrippina's cooperation to look forward to. With this noble girl's status, leaving the city with a few slaves, even the city gate guards wouldn't dare ask too many questions.

"Hopefully, there won't be any issues."

Victorido forced a faint smile. However, in Agrippina, she seemed to see a shadow of herself from yesterday, when she, too, had sacrificed everything for a boy, even though the future was uncertain and dangers lay ahead.

Octavius was just a slave, at most a renowned gladiator, but still a slave. In Rome, how could there be any interaction between slaves and nobles? Yet, Agrippina still did it, striving to help Octavius escape. Her dreams seemed unattainable. Thinking of this, Livia even considered helping them leave this city full of conspiracies and traps.

"Listen to me, you don't have to do this for me. You're Priscilla's daughter, the eldest of the Gaius family, with a prominent status, risking everything for me, a slave. Agrippina, go back."

In the underground prison, when Agrippina appeared in front of Henry again, his heart was filled with a warm and joyful feeling. However, after the excitement, Henry regained his composure. Agrippina, the daughter of a noble, risking so much to save a slave – if this were to spread, it would damage the reputation of the Gaius family and might even anger Caesar. Henry began to feel guilty for this girl's sacrifice; he shouldn't owe anyone such a huge favor.

"…"

Agrippina didn't respond but ordered her servant to dress up Henry. Then, she opened an exquisitely crafted suitcase, wooden with gemstone inlays. This was evidently a luxury item of the nobility, Agrippina's personal luggage.

Henry immediately understood her plan.

This clever girl intended to place the slave in front of her into her suitcase, then openly traverse the streets of Rome, bypassing inspections with her status. With such a prominent identity, even the magistrate wouldn't dare search Agrippina's luggage.

"Stay quiet inside later, don't make a sound, don't move recklessly. When we're outside the city gates, in a safe area, I'll open the suitcase and let you out."

Chapter 14

Agrippina stood there, calmly telling Henry. Her face still carried a touch of innocence, reddened by the prolonged exertion. Seeing this scene, Henry felt guilty. The sediment of time seemed to unfold before them, just like yesterday.

Not knowing how long he had embraced Agrippina, this moment felt eternal. Agrippina's departure left him dumbfounded, as time seemed to come to a standstill.

Now, he was a fugitive slave, without identity. Octavius had already been executed in the city; there was no legendary gladiator named Octavius anymore.

On a dark path outside Rome, everything was pitch black.

Chapter 15

"Halt, show me your travel permit."

Traversing from Rome towards the north, Henry proceeded cautiously, fearing to reveal any suspicious signs. From clothing to accessories, and even luggage, he chose the attire of a Roman knight to infiltrate the city. However, unlike previous years, this year saw a significant presence of Roman troops stationed on the trade route to Gaul.

Perhaps it was due to Caesar launching the Gallic War, causing a sudden tension in relations between Rome and Gaul. From what Henry knew before his time travel, not all Gallic tribes opposed Rome in the early stages of Caesar's Gallic War. Two major Celtic tribes near the Roman provinces – the Aedui and the Sequani – were allies of Rome.

One Celtic tribe, one Sequani tribe.

Chapter 15

Henry hadn't anticipated that anyone, regardless of who they were, needed a pass to enter or exit the Roman border.

"Brother, look..."

At the gate of the camp, with not many people around, Henry walked directly toward a Roman soldier checking passing pedestrians. Then, he discreetly handed a bag full of heavy coins to the guard.

The soldier's expression turned lecherous, but he was helpless. In this unfamiliar place, facing such a dilemma, one could only seek help humbly.

However, the guard seemed unmoved, perhaps because the money was too little or, during wartime, Caesar's soldiers dared not be corrupt. In any case, whether bribing or not, this action exposed Henry. He became the target of all soldiers. No need for inspection; everyone knew this person was attempting to cross the border, and detaining him for interrogation was just a matter of time.

"Seize him!"

The gatekeeper soldier immediately grabbed Henry around the waist. Before he could react, another guard standing by the gate swiftly joined. Within the camp, several Roman soldiers closer to Henry quickly surrounded him. Even with great skills, escaping at this moment was impossible.

Seeing the initially calm expression of the guard turning into anger, Henry knew he was in trouble. But escaping was impossible; there were guards on the wooden walls, armed with spears that could be thrown at any moment. Even if these Roman soldiers had the skill level of a language arts teacher, there were archers on the tower. In this environment, escape was simply impossible.

Therefore, Henry stopped struggling, waiting for this group of clumsy Roman soldiers to approach.

A few minutes later, a tall Roman officer walked over. From his decorations and the transverse crest on his helmet, there was no doubt he was a centurion, a legionary officer often seen in literary works and movies. However, just as Henry was preparing to smile and greet this burly centurion, he received a punch.

In this era, civilians had little status, especially a civilian attempting to cross the border. The centurion held Henry down and brought him to a nearby interrogation camp.

Inside the large tent, there weren't many people. Although called an interrogation camp, it was essentially the chief centurion's office. A few simple bookshelves, a plain wooden bed, a rough table, and two short wooden chairs were all the furniture in the centurion's office.

When Henry was brought in by the guards, there was no demand to kneel; he was just bound and made to sit on a small stool. The guards didn't remain standing either; they directly exited. It seemed this centurion had great confidence in dealing

Chapter 15

with a fugitive.

"Name."

The centurion sat at his desk, commencing the rough interrogation. Roman centurions usually had low cultural literacy, responsible only for managing a century of soldiers, and knew a lot about each soldier's situation. They had to charge ahead on the battlefield, make corresponding commands according to the situation. This was a high-risk military position; wealthy people generally avoided participating, and the poor had limited educational opportunities.

The centurion's first question made Henry feel awkward. In reality, he couldn't tell the centurion his true name in Rome because once someone knew, the gladiator who had once murdered Lucius Quinctius was still alive, it would surely cause a huge uproar. And it would lead to being recaptured by Rome, jeopardizing Agrippina. He couldn't use Octavius because he had already been executed in the city. Using Gaius was too risky, possibly stirring up family hatred. As for Marcus, it was also a name he couldn't mention; otherwise, it would endanger another family member.

In a desperate situation, Henry casually reported a Roman name – Lucius Aelius.

"Lucius Aelius, you are suspected of illegal border crossing. Speak up, what are you doing, running to the territory of the barbarians in the north?"

Centurion Marcus Flavius, sitting on his wooden desk, acted like a thug, occasionally chewing on nuts. Although perhaps this was true before joining the legion, he was now a military officer in a rather high-risk position.

"Actually, I am not illegally crossing the border, respected officer. In fact, I am just a merchant, looking to do a small business of selling wine in Gaul."

Lucius Aelius (well, another new name) pretended to look innocent. Considering his previous performance, combined with Lucius Aelius's demeanor, the centurion actually began to believe him. But soon, this centurion named Marcus Flavius regained his composure.

"Merchant? I've never seen a merchant venture alone into Gaul for the wine trade without attendants or slaves."

Marcus Flavius's expression grew increasingly fierce, his angry gaze almost tearing Lucius Aelius into pieces. However, Lucius Aelius was indifferent; for someone who had slaughtered countless people in the arena, perhaps even beasts were beneath notice, let alone an ordinary centurion.

"Attendants and slaves can be bought. I have enough money to purchase twenty slaves as companions and even hire an entire fleet of wagons. Roman merchants trading abroad are not obligated to bring attendants and slaves. In this era, if a trading caravan is too large and dresses too luxuriously, it may attract the attention of barbarians and bandits, right?"

Chapter 15

Lucius Aelius was quick-witted, and mentally resilient. For a moment, even the centurion seemed to believe him. But soon, Marcus Flavius regained his composure.

"Lucius Aelius, fine, even if what you say is true, without proper documents, you still can't pass through here. Now, go back to wherever you came from."

After saying this, Marcus Flavius spat the nuts from his mouth into the trash bin. Lucius Aelius felt fortunate to have passed the first round of inspection, tightened the tag on his shoulder, and prepared to leave. However, this subconscious action caught the centurion's attention.

"Halt! Show me your shoulder, let me see."

Marcus Flavius shouted, causing Lucius Aelius to even consider drawing his sword and fleeing. However, he couldn't ride a horse, and even if he took this centurion as a hostage, he couldn't escape the camp.

Claudius Severus, prepare for another round of slavery, he thought, closing his eyes. At this moment, he finally understood why people often sought spiritual comfort through prayer, even when they knew misfortune was imminent but powerless to change it.

"Slave! Damn it, I should have known you're a slave."

Marcus Flavius uncovered the linen on Lucius Aelius's shoulder, and in the next moment, this strong centurion's expression turned furious. Not only did he fail to realize the illegal intruder before him was a slave, but he also felt manipulated by him. If his soldiers found out, how would they view their centurion?

In anger, Marcus Flavius knocked Lucius Aelius down with a punch. But Lucius Aelius didn't dare resist; resistance would only invite more beatings and abuse. In ancient Rome, slaves were like livestock, with no status, subject to exploitation.

"Damn it, you swine. Slaves, move faster."

In the pouring rain, the Roman supply convoy was stuck in the muddy road, despite having the world's most advanced roads within Rome's borders. However, once outside Rome, the roads connecting various provinces were rough and poorly constructed mud paths. Once it rained, it was easy for the wagon wheels to get stuck in muddy pits.

Claudius Severus, along with a large group of slaves, around two hundred in total, was now moving grain from the wagons. Since Marcus Flavius discovered he was a slave during the last incident, this stern and irritable Roman centurion threw Claudius Severus into the ranks of the slaves. He was now responsible for unloading the supplies and grain that arrived at the border every day.

Of course, this grain wasn't meant for the two or three hundred people in the camp but was intended as provisions for the large armies on the front lines. Claudius Severus found it strange; according to his historical knowledge from before his time

Chapter 15

travel, during Caesar's conquest of Gaul, most of the grain was supplied by the surrounding tribes. The Gaulish tribes sympathetic to Rome would send food to the Roman legions' camps, rather than relying on long-distance transport from Rome like this.

Imagine a convoy loaded with provisions and supplies, heading to the legion's front lines. Even if it departs from the Roman province in southern France closest to Gaul, the journey is laborious and costly. By the time the convoy reaches the legion, nearly half of the provisions may have been depleted, especially on a day like today with torrential rain. If the rain persists for several days, there's a risk of the supplies turning moldy.

Additionally, the personnel in the convoy would consume a portion of the provisions during the journey. So, transporting provisions from within Rome seems highly impractical. Claudius Severus contemplated raising this question, but given the centurion's volatile temper, he knew the answer wouldn't come from a lowly slave. Besides, the junior centurion might not be aware himself.

"Damn it, scum, get up. Don't tell me you can't stand."

In the pouring rain, while the wagon wheels were still stuck in the mud, an elderly and frail slave fell painfully to the ground. Marcus Flavius immediately approached, wielding the short staff that symbolized his authority over a century, and stood over the elderly man. Clearly unable to continue, the old man lay there in agony, covered in mud under the rain.

However, the centurion paid no attention to the suffering weakling. Instead, he walked over and roughly pulled the old man up by his collar, forcing him to stand again. Claudius Severus could even see the old man's emaciated legs, worn out from prolonged illness and exhaustion.

"Stand up, get back into line, or I'll run you through right now."

Claudius Severus stood behind another wagon, watching this scene unfold. Initially, he thought the centurion might show some compassion by offering the old man a piece of bread or some water to alleviate his weariness. However, Marcus Flavius's reaction was quite the opposite. In fact, as he spoke, the gleaming Roman short sword was already at the old man's neck. In Rome, officers and soldiers didn't consider slaves as human.

Damn it!

Claudius Severus cursed inwardly, realizing the outcome he should have expected. Though reluctant to witness such brutal scenes, he was powerless at this moment. If he spoke up for the old man now, he might become the centurion's next target. In the Roman military, especially during Caesar's conquest of Gaul, Rome had an abundance of slaves, and their value sometimes equaled that of an axe. If he stepped forward now, not only would he fail to help the old man, but he might also become an example for the Roman centurion to demonstrate his authority.

Enduring immense pain, Claudius Severus turned his face away,

Chapter 15

unwilling to witness this barbaric cruelty.

The old slave trembled under the centurion's sword, and in the next moment, blood stained the muddy ground at Marcus Flavius's feet.

This was a savage era. Despite representing the most advanced and glorious civilization of this time, Rome's social structure, built on slavery, was still filled with many brutal and violent scenes. Claudius Severus had known about this situation before his time travel, but facing it now, he couldn't help but feel profound sorrow.

Yet, Rome's conquest of the surrounding tribes might not necessarily be a bad thing. Although slavery was cruel, knowing that the northern barbarian tribes were still sacrificing live humans to their gods made it clear which side he should stand on.

The convoy struggled until evening to pull all the wagons out of the muddy water pits. By this time, the torrential rain had ceased.

After setting up camp, Marcus Flavius stormed into the crowd of soldiers, sitting by the blazing campfire, cursing the wretched weather they encountered today. Obviously, such adverse weather would delay the supply convoy's arrival at the front lines even further. Marcus Flavius had no idea what kind of punishment awaited him from the legion commander, but as long as it didn't involve docking his pay or receiving a few lashes, he didn't mind.

Several slaves huddled in a corner, sleeping like exhausted mules, completely motionless. Indeed, the day's physical labor had left them drained.

"You're new here?"

A seemingly frail slave approached, sitting next to Claudius Severus. Apparently, like Claudius Severus, he was one of the few insomniacs among the slaves.

"Yes, you don't seem like someone accustomed to physical labor?"

Claudius Severus squinted and asked, observing his friendly-looking companion. His delicate skin and slender physique immediately struck him as unusual. This man should have been engaged in creative work, perhaps a copywriter, yet he ended up in the ranks of laboring slaves.

"Yes, I came out of Adrianople just two months ago, dragged into the slave ranks."

"What crime did you commit to be enslaved?"

Claudius Severus asked curiously, simultaneously studying this unfortunate stranger from a distant province. These people, who had never known each other, were now gathered together, sharing their tragic pasts.

"I used to live in Adrianople, in a modest apartment, leading a humble yet happy life with my wife. We also had a daughter…"

Chapter 15

Before the stars descended, under the moonlight shining in the Roman military camp, in an atmosphere of calm and serenity, Quintus Marcellus, also a slave like Claudius Severus, sat beside him, recounting his bitter past. Slaves might not always be born as slaves; many times, debtors and criminals would descend from free citizens, losing their freedom. Quintus Marcellus was one such case, having a wife who accumulated gambling debts and borrowed from loan sharks. When the creditors came knocking, Quintus Marcellus suffered the same fate. Now, this frail man who had

Chapter 16

"When will the war ever end?"

In the Roman centurion camp shrouded in nightfall, people gradually dispersed into their respective tents, leaving only a few old soldiers gathered around a campfire, complaining about this endless war. Centurion Marcus Flavius was particularly prominent, leading the charge in cursing several Roman legion commanders overseeing the Gaul expedition. Except for Caesar, almost every legion commander had received his share of curses.

In reality, the past two years of campaigning in Gaul had brought tangible benefits to many, such as abundant spoils of war, money, and slaves. However, most of these advantages flowed into the pockets of high-ranking commanders and the wealthy, leaving little opportunity for the common soldiers to return home, let alone enjoy the improved life these riches

Chapter 16

could bring.

"After returning to Rome, I want a hundred courtesans and add twenty slave girls; then my household will be complete."

"Let it go, Titus Cornelius. Your wife probably couldn't wait to kick you out long ago."

Drunk soldiers began boasting about the brighter future awaiting them once the war ended. However, no one knew what would happen the next moment, who would fall in battle on the northern lands?

Late at night, as slaves lay down to rest, Claudius Severus sat quietly on the side, listening to soldiers' complaints and fantasies about the future.

Although the centurion in charge of the Roman supply convoy shouldn't be drinking, out in the wilderness, centurions were kings, and military regulations meant little to them.

Suddenly, the tranquility of the deep night was shattered by a series of war cries as barbarian warriors stealthily appeared on the edge of the camp.

"Ooh."

A signaler tried to blow the horn, but a Gallic warrior silently severed his throat. In the chaos, Claudius Severus saw Marcus Flavius rushing out of his tent, wielding a short sword, issuing orders. However, the battlefield had descended into chaos, with many Roman soldiers already falling under the swords of barbarian warriors.

Slaves fled frantically, facing death. Claudius Severus sat by a pile of grass, suddenly awakened again.

"Get up, soldier, damn it."

In the melee, Claudius Severus saw Marcus Flavius charging towards him, tearing the ropes off his hands.

Once freed, Claudius Severus picked up a Gallic weapon and plunged into the battlefield; this was his only chance.

Blood splattered, and Claudius Severus returned to the gladiatorial scenes, wielding a long sword, displaying adept combat skills.

"Roar."

Claudius Severus went into a bloodlust frenzy, unstoppable. Marcus Flavius was also locked in a fierce battle with Gallic warriors. With Claudius Severus assisting, the situation in the camp gradually improved.

"Centurion, give me a sword; I'm a gladiator, I can fight!"

Claudius Severus shouted, and Marcus Flavius looked at him, immediately cutting his ropes without hesitation.

Claudius Severus swung the long sword, agilely maneuvering

Chapter 16

among the Gallic warriors, showcasing the unique skills of a gladiator.

"Roar."

The Gallic warriors began to retreat, and in the camp, the number of defeated Gallic warriors by Claudius Severus kept increasing. This night, they successfully repelled the ambush.

Chapter 17

4. Emergency Conscription

In the centurion camp after the fierce battle, bodies of various kinds were strewn everywhere—Romans, barbarians, and some unlucky slaves lay among them. The remaining survivors began to clean up the bodies lying in the camp. Regardless, they had to spend the night here, replenishing their spirits for the journey ahead.

The scent of battle lingered in the centurion camp, bodies scattered on the ground—Romans and barbarians alike, along with some unfortunate slaves, silently immersed in the long night. The survivors started clearing the aftermath of the battle. Although blood still stained the ground, they could only spend the night on this bloody land, waiting for the dawn of the next day.

In this era of war, the Roman soldiers who had just been

Chapter 17

discussing post-war life moments ago had now become cold corpses on the ground. The brutality of war destroyed all beautiful imaginations.

"Claudius Severus."

Centurion Marcus Flavius finished counting the number of troops and walked up to Claudius Severus.

Perhaps it was in the recent intense battle that Claudius Severus displayed exceptional courage, maybe even saving the centurion's life at a crucial moment. Now, Marcus Flavius' attitude towards Claudius Severus had softened, gaining a measure of respect. However, deep down, the centurion faced a conflict because Claudius Severus was, after all, a slave. The centurion was not accustomed to engaging in equal conversations with slaves, despite Claudius Severus having just saved his life, arguably rescuing the entire squad.

"Obey your orders, Centurion."

Claudius Severus stood before the centurion, prepared to hand over the Celtic sword stained with enemy blood.

"Slave, I won't dwell on this, but today you showed the bravery and resilience of a Roman. Now, with only thirty-four of us left, clean up tonight, report tomorrow, you'll temporarily join our ranks."

For Claudius Severus, this was a precious opportunity. Not because of joining the Roman legion but a chance to establish merit on the battlefield, perhaps altering the fate of a slave. Agrippina awaited him in Rome, fueling all his struggles.

"Hope everything goes smoothly tomorrow."

As Claudius Severus anticipated a promising future, Marcus Flavius cursed his way back to his tent, inspecting damaged tools and wagons. Clearly, the recent barbarian attack wasn't just about slaughter; destroying supplies was also one of their objectives.

"Brothers, unfortunately, I have to inform you that tomorrow we need to detour to the territory of the Sequani people. We'll repair our supplies there, rent some horses, then continue. Damn it, the barbarians not only killed our comrades but also damaged our supplies and horses."

Claudius Severus, just asked to report early the next morning by the centurion, was now part of the impromptu soldiers' meeting.

The mission was to detour to the town of the Sequani, but the original plan was to pass through the territory of the Helvetii to reach the frontline camp of the Seventh Legion as quickly as possible. However, due to the unfriendly nature of the Helvetii towards Rome and the fact that the nearest town was at least five miles away, Marcus Flavius decided to go to the Sequani town first and then head north to the Seventh Legion's camp.

No one voiced any objections because in this unit, Marcus Flavius' words held unmatched authority. However, as everyone

Chapter 17

prepared to march, there was a low murmur of dissent from behind the meeting table. When everyone turned around, they found Claudius Severus, who had been quietly standing in the corner, bearing the slave mark on his chest.

"Centurion, I think this is a bit risky."

Everyone present was astonished to see a slave directly opposing the centurion's command. Moreover, nobody noticed when this slave silently entered. At this moment, Claudius Severus realized that Marcus Flavius hadn't introduced himself to everyone because, in this unit, the opinions of new recruits weren't valued, and he was unaware.

Even Centurion Marcus Flavius himself was momentarily stunned, his eyes reddening as he asked, "What objection do you have, new recruit?"

Everyone present widened their eyes, anticipating the centurion's reprimand of this new recruit.

"Gladiator, your concerns are unnecessary. The Sequani people have peacefully coexisted with our Roman legion for many years. Stepping onto this Gallic land, I've never engaged in war with them. They treat us like docile lambs, only providing what the Roman legion needs, without resisting their masters."

The Roman soldiers inside the tents expected the centurion to explode, but Marcus Flavius surprisingly remained calm, explaining his views on the Sequani people. Perhaps it was because Claudius Severus had just saved his life, Marcus Flavius didn't roar at him as he did with other slaves. The remnants of the battle still lingered, but Centurion Marcus Flavius chose not to camp outside the city; instead, he led the convoy directly into the Sequani town. After settling the wagons and baggage in a moderately-sized tavern, the centurion, accompanied by the Roman soldiers, grandiosely entered the establishment. It was only then that Claudius Severus realized the centurion had always wanted to enter this town to while away time with local women.

"How can this man be a centurion?" Claudius Severus murmured, following behind the group.

Claudius Severus got the answer to the question that had been bothering him. Upon entering Sequani territory, through conversations with Roman soldiers and local residents, he learned that the entire Gaul region had suffered severe flooding and locust infestations this year, dealing a significant blow to the tribes supplying food to the Roman legion. To sustain their livelihoods, some legion commanders had no choice but to seek provisions from Rome with Caesar's approval, explaining the previous extensive journeys of the Roman century to transport supplies.

With shortages in food, the Roman legions were facing tough times. In this predominantly agricultural region of Gaul, the residents were also troubled. Although the people's surface lives seemed to be getting by, the entire town was shrouded in a gloomy atmosphere, and Claudius Severus sensed an indescribable unease.

Chapter 17

In the tavern, Marcus Flavius strode confidently towards the Celtic woman at the bar, a plump lady smearing inferior honey on herself, attempting to attract passing merchants and forest hunters.

"Beauty, it's been a few months, and you're still so enchanting." Marcus Flavius unabashedly approached, lifting the chubby landlady.

Claudius Severus sat in the corner, observing the scene. Roman soldiers occupied the best spots in the tavern, getting intimate with local women. While such behavior disgusted Claudius Severus, he was well aware of the inconsistent quality of troops within the legion.

Several Gaul women approached Claudius Severus in the corner. "No, thank you," Claudius Severus kept declining, but these women were unwilling to give up. In the end, Claudius Severus had to claim he had no money on him to escape the attention of a few persistent women.

The centurion descended from upstairs, the sound of military boots drawing the soldiers' attention. "Pack up, we're leaving." This caught everyone off guard, soldiers ceasing their intimate interactions with women and turning their gazes toward the centurion. In Claudius Severus' eyes, the centurion seemed to have been aware of the situation here for a while.

By evening, the Roman soldiers left the Sequani town, surprising all the Gauls. The carriages were ready, everything seemed rushed. As the centurion walked out of the tavern's gate, he gave Claudius Severus a meaningful look, indicating that there might be hidden dangers behind this departure. The entire scene was unpredictable, resembling a march of the Roman century, with everything happening casually.

Chapter 18

The echoes of battle still lingered as Roman Centurion Marcus Flavius chose not to camp outside the city but instead directed the convoy straight into the town of the Sequani people. After settling the wagons and baggage in a moderately-sized tavern, Centurion Marcus Flavius led the Roman soldiers grandiosely into the establishment. It was at this moment that Claudius Severus understood that the centurion had been wanting to enter this town to spend time with local women.

"How can this man be a centurion?" Claudius Severus muttered, following behind the group.

Claudius Severus finally got the answer to the question that had been bothering him. Upon entering Sequani territory, through conversations with Roman soldiers and local residents, he learned that the entire Gaul region had suffered severe flooding and locust infestations this year, dealing a significant blow to the tribes supplying food to the Roman legion. To sustain their livelihoods, some legion commanders had no choice but to seek provisions from Rome with Caesar's approval, explaining the previous extensive journeys of the Roman century to transport supplies.

With shortages in food, the Roman legions were facing tough times. In this predominantly agricultural region of Gaul, the residents were also troubled. Although the people's surface lives seemed to be getting by, the entire town was shrouded in a gloomy atmosphere, and Claudius Severus sensed an indescribable unease.

In the tavern, Marcus Flavius strode confidently towards the Celtic woman at the bar, a plump lady smearing inferior honey on herself, attempting to attract passing merchants and forest hunters.

"Little beauty, it's been a few months, and you're still so enchanting." Marcus Flavius unabashedly approached, lifting the chubby landlady.

Claudius Severus sat in the corner, observing the scene. Roman soldiers occupied the best spots in the tavern, getting intimate with local women. While such behavior disgusted Claudius Severus, he was well aware of the inconsistent quality of troops within the legion.

Several Gaul women approached Claudius Severus in the

Chapter 18

corner. "No, thank you," Claudius Severus kept declining, but these women were unwilling to give up. In the end, Claudius Severus had to claim he had no money on him to escape the attention of a few persistent women.

The centurion descended from upstairs, the sound of military boots drawing the soldiers' attention. "Pack up, we're leaving." This caught everyone off guard, soldiers ceasing their intimate interactions with women and turning their gazes toward the centurion. In Claudius Severus' eyes, the centurion seemed to have been aware of the situation here for a while.

By evening, the Roman soldiers left the Sequani town, surprising all the Gauls. The carriages were ready, everything seemed rushed. As the centurion walked out of the tavern's gate, he gave Claudius Severus a meaningful look, indicating that there might be hidden dangers behind this departure. The entire scene was unpredictable, resembling a march of the Roman century, with everything happening casually.

The slaves had grown accustomed to their master's cruel treatment, but one day, when the master ceased the abuse, they saw it as a benevolence.

Once, Claudius Severus found this perverse psychology challenging to comprehend. However, as night fell, Marcus Flavius distributed weapons to the emaciated slaves and told them that if they fought valiantly tonight, they might earn their freedom and escape their slave status. The slaves erupted with excitement, although in reality, Marcus Flavius did not have the authority. He could only write a letter to the legion commander, detailing the exceptional performance of these slaves during the escort of supplies. Whether to pardon their slave status depended on the legion commander's decision. Centurion Marcus Flavius merely submitted a simple letter of recommendation.

Yet, even this faint glimmer of hope filled the slaves with anticipation, as if they could glimpse a future of freedom, no longer oppressed, possessing dignity and liberty.

Claudius Severus felt a wave of sadness. Fortunately, he was now a member of the Roman century, albeit a temporary conscript. Yet, in the eyes of the soldiers around him, Claudius Severus could discern the expectations they held for him. After all, in the recent Gallic ambush a few days ago, it was he who valiantly fought the barbarians, successfully repelling them.

To prevent the Gauls from pursuing during the day and launching a night attack, Marcus Flavius ordered all soldiers not to light any fires, lurking in the haystacks. Though tents were still pitched in the camp, the bedding was filled with cotton.

To make the entire camp look more ordinary, Marcus Flavius arranged several slaves to stand on the wooden fence, dressed in Roman infantry attire, pretending to guard the camp. Although these slaves might become the first targets of an attack, they had no choice.

After everything was set up, the centurion led the men to start their vigil.

Chapter 18

Like previous ambushes, the Roman military camp was eerily quiet in the first half of the night, as if everyone was immersed in a dream. Even the slaves standing on the wooden wall were motionless, resembling sculptures, although upon closer inspection, many slaves remained tense, with some even sweating in fear.

The scent of slaughter permeated the air, but the slaves remained oblivious.

It wasn't until the first barbarian climbed the wooden wall that everyone breathed a sigh of relief. Throughout the night's vigil, they waited for the centurion to lead the charge. In the first half of the night, it was agreed that everyone must remain in place until Marcus Flavius charged out of the haystacks.

Time passed, and every second felt incredibly long. Legion infantry hid in the haystacks, watching the tattooed barbarian soldiers pass by.

Everyone held their breath.

Swoosh.

When the barbarians entered the tents, the counter-ambush began.

As Marcus Flavius stood up, hurling the first javelin, more Roman soldiers charged out from the haystacks. For a moment, the once quiet camp echoed with thunderous cries of battle.

Claudius Severus leaped out from the last haystack, pouncing on the nearest barbarian warrior. Before the barbarian could even turn around, Claudius Severus's short sword cut through his throat. In an instant, blood gushed out, staining Claudius Severus's hands red. Although such brutal slaughter was not new to him, it remained shocking. Claudius Severus's heart raced again, not out of nervousness but the rhythmic pulse of combat, an involuntary physiological response.

What started as a sneak attack turned into an ambush, resulting in more casualties than a frontal assault.

Some bold slaves, striving for their freedom, rushed out into the darkness. As Roman soldiers clashed with the barbarians, these slaves, once mistreated by Roman officers, now targeted the backs and thighs of the barbarians with daggers and short swords.

Due to Marcus Flavius's effective psychological work, he told these slaves that the Gauls also enjoyed mistreating slaves, making them do their bidding. Moreover, barbarians had the tradition of sacrificing live humans to their gods. Although Claudius Severus knew that such practices might only be done by more northern Germanic people, the Gauls' level of civilization shouldn't be so barbaric.

Sounds of weapon clashes and barbarian cries intertwined in a chaotic scene, blood splattering like red wine across the entire field. Claudius Severus thrust his short sword into a Gaul's throat, and then the barbarian clutched Claudius Severus's shoulders, convulsing before collapsing, blood splattering on

Chapter 18

Claudius Severus's face.

"To the wooden wall!"

Marcus Flavius shouted, and half of the legion infantry rushed towards the camp's defensive structures. This time, they wouldn't let any raiders escape.

Several Gaul attackers tried to flee the camp and, just before charging out of the gate, found themselves trapped inside this small Roman encampment.

Dozens of Roman infantry raised short javelins, aiming at these Gauls.

"Damn it, Tiberius, translate."

The barbarians laid down their weapons, but Marcus Flavius couldn't understand what they were saying. Earlier, when entering the Gallic inn, many Gauls spoke Latin, interacting with the Romans. However, these Gauls attacking the camp might not have used Latin at all but spoke their own tribal language. Marcus Flavius called upon his translator from within the ranks.

"He says they didn't attack us on purpose but were coerced by other tribes, forcing them to launch the assault."

Tiberius approached the centurion, translating the explanation of these Gauls into fluent language.

"FUCK, do they think I'm a fool to believe that?"

After hearing this, Marcus Flavius went straight forward, punching one of the Gauls, leaving him knocked out. The remaining ones, witnessing the Roman centurion mistreating a prisoner, thought about resisting but found Roman spears tightly gripped in the hands of the soldiers.

"Ask them which tribe ordered them here."

After the beating of the prisoners, Marcus Flavius ordered his translator to continue the conversation with these Gallic captives.

It turned out that the centurion had only sought to vent his anger by physically assaulting the prisoners. Claudius Severus stood aside, watching the scene unfold, unable to comprehend the actions of the Roman centurion.

Chapter 19

"The Germanic people?"

Centurion Marcus Flavius was astonished by the startling news from the captives, a rare occurrence for the usually bold and rough centurion. However, Claudius Severus had a deeper understanding of the Germanic people mentioned by the Gallic prisoners.

They were a warlike tribe, bloodthirsty and brutal, skilled in the torture of captives. Their lives revolved around hunting, and the forest was their habitat. They showed no fear of pain in battle, crazily slaughtering every enemy in front of them. Germanic men almost never participated in household chores, leaving all labor to the women. Throughout the year, their focus was solely on one thing—warfare. In times of peace, Germanic men gathered in groups, engaging in revelry and friendly combat to showcase their manhood. However, when war erupted, men from all Germanic tribes united, pouncing on their enemies like beasts. Even during the height of the Roman Empire, these northern European barbarians remained unconquered.

If the information from the Gallic prisoners was accurate, this intelligence would be crucial and invaluable for the Roman legion.

After a moment of contemplation, Marcus Flavius summoned two skilled reconnaissance riders and, riding the Gallic horses, hurried to the front lines of the Seventh Legion to inform the legion commander, Acco, that the Germanic people were about to launch a counterattack.

"Quintus Marcellus, Lucius Antonius, Decimus, gather the remaining weapons and load them onto the carts."

"Aelia, Sabina, handle these prisoners."

"The rest of you, follow me. We're setting out. Damn it, why do we always run into trouble?"

After dispatching the riders to report to the front lines, Marcus Flavius swiftly issued three commands, and the soldiers moved rapidly as instructed by the centurion. Only Claudius Severus raised another question—

"Centurion, these prisoners have provided valuable intelligence. Do we still need to execute them?"

Chapter 19

Previously, cruel interrogations of Gallic prisoners might have been understandable, but this time, when the Gallic prisoners had confessed the truth, Claudius Severus found it hard to comprehend and accept the centurion's insistence on executing them. As a modern man, such treatment of prisoners seemed excessively inhumane and devoid of morality.

Claudius Severus's questioning drew attention from the entire camp...

In the Roman legion, superior orders were followed without question during wartime, and soldiers dared not utter the word "no." However, Claudius Severus, a gladiator by origin, repeatedly questioned the authority of the centurion. Even in the face of consecutive barbarian attacks and heavy casualties, Marcus Flavius felt the impulse to draw his sword and end this "talkative" gladiator.

"They are my prisoners, and how to deal with them is my affair. You're just a slave, a soldier, with no right to interfere with the centurion's orders. Understand?"

Marcus Flavius roared angrily, striding directly to Claudius Severus. The two faced each other like two wild beasts about to tear each other apart, eyes filled with provocation and anger. In the end, Marcus Flavius did not take action against Claudius Severus. After all, in this situation, a gladiator's combat prowess could match that of ten legionary infantrymen, and coupled with Claudius Severus's previous performance of defeating numerous Gauls in combat, the gladiator's strength was beyond doubt. If not for such a unique circumstance, Marcus Flavius might have already dealt with this "chattering" gladiator on the road.

"FUCK, is ancient warfare always this cruel?"

After the dispute, Claudius Severus could not prevent the centurion from executing the Gallic prisoners. He shouldered his belongings alone, joining the column of marching soldiers.

In Rome, at the home of Gaius Octavius—

"Mother, please listen to my explanation."

Agrippina was held by Priscilla's handmaidens, tears flowing, trying to persuade her mother. However, in Priscilla's eyes, rescuing a slave guilty of a capital offense, especially in collusion with Pompey's subordinate Valerius Aurelius, was an unforgivable mistake.

Risking the reputation of the Gaius family, the daughter had committed an act that, in Priscilla's view, was an irredeemable error. In this delicate moment, even the slightest mistake could lead to the faction's fracture. The Senate was actively sowing discord between Pompey and Caesar, and at this time, the daughter had made such an unwise move.

However, the now calm Priscilla also understood her daughter's feelings. Noble marriages were devoid of freedom, often forced unions with unseen individuals, solely for the sake of political advantage.

Chapter 19

Priscilla, like all women, had once been a young girl, unable to be with the man of her dreams and could only gaze from afar. Therefore, when Agrippina behaved so recklessly, Priscilla's heart was also filled with contradictions. However, she still couldn't forgive her daughter. The harsh reality taught this great mother that you cannot choose your birth; everything must conform to society.

"Agrippina, my daughter, I understand your feelings. But as I've told you before, you are a noble, and Octavius is a slave. You two cannot be together unless he gains civilian status and Roman citizenship. However, even if he achieves that later, it will be extremely difficult for you two to be together. You are not an ordinary noblewoman; you are a daughter of the Gaius family, and Caesar is your uncle. Your lineage dictates that you cannot choose your marriage, just like me."

Priscilla approached, wiping away the tears from her daughter's eyes. At this moment, as a mother, Priscilla's heart was undoubtedly in pain. She didn't want to see her daughter hurt, but she had to teach her the harsh reality.

...

Agrippina fell silent, silently crying in place. Like an injured kitten, she curled up alone in a corner, licking her wounds. Falling in love with someone might only take a day, one night, while forgetting someone could take several years, even a lifetime. Agrippina was like that, but she didn't know how her lover, the gladiator she had rescued from the underground prison in Rome, was doing now. Was he still thinking about her? He had promised to return with glory and triumph, but, under Priscilla's guidance, all of it had turned into a dream, a fleeting illusion…

The rapid marching throughout the day had exhausted the soldiers' last ounce of energy. The Roman legion infantry, despite harsh physical training on the front lines and the reforms of Marius making them jokingly called "faster than mules," faced the undeniable importance of the Germanic invasion. If mishandled, the two years of Caesar's conquest in Gaul might go up in smoke.

The non-stop marching had continued until evening, and this inhumane way of moving forward had pushed the soldiers to their physical limits. After several days of forced marches, many soldiers had blisters on their feet. Marcus Flavius was forced to have the soldiers stop and rest for a while to alleviate the continuous impact on their bodies. However, he strictly prohibited making fires because the supply train had entered the territory of the Belgians. Unlike the previous friendly Segani and Edui, these barbarians were hostile to the Romans, merely suppressing the resistance of the local tribes because Caesar had arranged for two legions to be stationed here.

"For days, you've been praying to that small wooden carving. Tell me, is that your faith?"

Quintus Marcellus sat under a large tree, curiously asking Claudius Severus.

"No, that's my past."

Chapter 19

Quintus Marcellus's question prompted Claudius Severus to recall Agrippina, the girl he had longed for during his escape, far away. However, now those memories seemed like a beautiful yet elusive dream to him.

"She must be beautiful, to make you miss her every day. I see you holding that carving when you rest."

"Yes, more beautiful than Venus."

Claudius Severus spoke, his gaze unfocused, immersed in memories of the past. In that mountain villa, Agrippina wore a pristine dress, standing beside him. The night wind brushed through his hair, and her black hair was as enchanting as that of Eastern women.

"After the war is over, you two can be together."

Watching Claudius Severus's nostalgic expression, Quintus Marcellus felt a sense of loneliness. The slave in this legion, like Claudius Severus, had beautiful yet sad memories. Just as Quintus Marcellus had said during his first conversation with Claudius Severus, he longed to return to the past, to the time when his wife had not fallen, in Aretium, where they had a small apartment and lived a simple yet happy life.

"No, after the war, it's even harder for us to be together."

Claudius Severus turned to Quintus Marcellus. This statement left the Roman man even more confused.

"Why?"

"Because my lover is a noblewoman from Rome, and I was a slave before leaving there. Slaves and nobles cannot coexist. Unless war comes, I achieve merit on the battlefield, escape slavery, gain citizenship, only then there's a slim chance of reuniting with my lover."

Claudius Severus spoke with a face full of helplessness and bitterness.

A few days later, intense arguments erupted between two commanders in the camp of the Roman Seventh Legion. Everyone felt the need to verify the authenticity of the intelligence from Gallic prisoners, leading the commanders to decide to send a spy to the largest town in Belgium—Condrus, to gather the most accurate information. However, the issue of choosing a spy sparked a heated debate between the two commanders. Camulogenus believed that using a slave as a spy was extremely dangerous, while Acco argued that the legion should not entrust intelligence gathering to an inexperienced slave.

Ultimately, Claudius Severus was summoned to the commander's tent.

"Gladiator, this is a dangerous mission, and after much consideration, we've decided to have you carry it out. Venture into the heart of the barbarians, deliver the most accurate intelligence; your success will be Rome's glory. If successful, you'll gain freedom and citizenship."

Chapter 19

The first to receive Claudius Severus was Camulogenus, the commander of the Seventh Legion. His damp appearance and optimistic demeanor were well-received in the legion. However, Camulogenus's radical and adventurous attitude made him an unusual decision-maker in sending a slave as a spy. In everyone's mind, there were doubts about whether Claudius Severus could complete the mission.

In the small town of Bubul in Gaul, originally a city of the Belgians that surrendered to Caesar, it had now become a gathering place for Gauls resisting Rome. Claudius Severus had nothing before setting out, only borrowing one person from the Seventh Legion's commander Camulogenus, and that person was Quintus Marcellus. Claudius Severus told him that if the mission succeeded, they would both gain freedom after the war.

Initially, Camulogenus was reluctant to agree. As the commander of the Seventh Legion, he highly valued Claudius Severus for showing stronger combat abilities and psychological resilience than others during the escort of supply wagons. However, venturing into enemy territory was a formidable task not everyone could endure. Claudius Severus also had to take an inexperienced slave companion, and Camulogenus feared it would jeopardize the entire spy mission. Nevertheless, Claudius Severus had his reasons; he wanted to stage a play with Quintus Marcellus to better deceive the Gauls.

In the end, Camulogenus agreed. Acco, on the other hand, was sulking in the tent, unwilling to show his face, not wanting to witness this absurd scene.

In reality, after Claudius Severus left, the two legion commanders reached an agreement. Regardless of whether the slave brought back intelligence, the camp had to be strengthened to guard against the Germans.

Stepping into the Gaul town for the first time, Claudius Severus felt like he had walked into a gathering of beggars. This was a place near the northern Gaul tribes, with almost no trace of Roman civilization. The town resembled a maze, with low houses densely packed like refugee camps. The roads in Bubul twisted and turned like a giant spider web, making the city an inescapable maze.

Claudius Severus and Quintus Marcellus were bound by the Belgians. These Belgians, distrusting whether there were traitors among the Romans, bound the two Romans as spies.

"Look, Roman spies."

The leader of the barbarians shouted, and a punch came. Claudius Severus tasted the saltiness of blood on his lips. He had forgotten how many times he had been beaten in this era, but as long as he was alive, there was hope. Enduring the pain, Claudius Severus spat blood on the face of the barbarian who was beating him.

"You bastard…"

Then the stronger warrior became even more fierce in his beating.

Chapter 19

"Wait."

The Belgians bound Claudius Severus and Quintus Marcellus in the square of the town center, attracting the attention of many passing Gauls. Passing Gaulish merchants saw the scene.

"Are you Romans? Escaped from the Roman camp?"

A Gaulish merchant squeezed into the crowd, appearing to have a higher status among all the tribes, perhaps a noble Gaul. He stepped forward, and the barbarians stopped beating Claudius Severus. They stared at the merchant intently.

"Yes, damn it. How many times do I have to say it? Damn Gaulish pigs!"

Claudius Severus shouted loudly for the surrounding Gauls to hear. Although not everyone in the tribe understood Latin, those Gauls who did understand seemed hostile towards him. As for the standard English words, no one could comprehend.

"You don't need to interrogate them anymore; they are indeed slaves. I've seen this mark. Only the lowest and most unfree slaves have this brand. Moreover, branded on the chest, these two people will probably never get rid of this mark in their lives."

The Gaulish merchant carefully examined the mark on Claudius Severus's chest and then informed people from all the tribes around. However, the Gauls who captured Claudius Severus and Quintus Marcellus did not intend to believe the words of the merchant. Instead, they approached, ready to continue beating Claudius Severus.

"Enough, Yeruchenko. The enemy's enemy is our ally."

The Gaulish merchant shouted with authority, and the barbarian covered in Claudius Severus's blood stopped slightly. At the same time, he spat on Claudius Severus and Quintus Marcellus.

"Damn!"

In this era filled with chaos and warfare, it was the most profound experience in Claudius Severus's heart that the poor struggled to survive. But the mission was not yet complete, and he had to endure everything. He remembered a Chinese proverb: "Heaven imposes heavy responsibilities on those who are worthy of them. It withholds nothing from those who are diligent." Although it was just a comforting phrase, in the darkest moments, it became the last stronghold in people's hearts.

"Why were you so rude to them just now? Weren't we coming to seek refuge with these savages and gather intelligence? Isn't such a rude attitude asking for trouble?"

After being thrown into a stinking dungeon, Quintus Marcellus sat beside Claudius Severus, feeling puzzled about the situation.

"Brother, my good friend, this is the place you need to learn. To successfully infiltrate the enemy, you must first dispel their

Chapter 19

suspicions. We are outsiders, and the first reaction of these savages is that we are Roman spies trying to infiltrate them for information. So, their initial rough treatment of us is normal. At this time, if we show a humble attitude, it's easy for them to suspect that we intentionally want to blend in to gather information. So, at this moment, the more we can't show the desire to stay, the more we can't show the eagerness to integrate into them. I cursed them because they beat us. At this time, a normal person's reaction to being beaten should be to treat it with the mindset of an ordinary wanderer, not approaching with a purpose. This way, it's less likely to arouse suspicion."

Claudius Severus explained with a smile while sitting in the smelly underground dungeon. Although Quintus Marcellus wasn't very clever, he quickly understood Claudius Severus's intentions. At the same time, this native Roman couldn't help but admire the gladiator in front of him from the bottom of his heart. No wonder

Camulogenus chose him for such a dangerous mission; Claudius Severus's thoughts and insight were indeed superior to ordinary infantry.

Chapter 20

In the small Gaul town of Bubul, where the Belgians had once surrendered to Caesar, they were now in rebellion against Roman rule. Claudius Severus and Quintus Marcellus became new members of this city, with their first job being to tend to livestock, transport fodder, and clean pigsties. In the foul-smelling environment, the two stepped into the farm of this Gaul tribe.

These once despised tasks now became a part of Claudius Severus's daily life. Compared to Roman farms, the pigsties and chicken coops here were dirtier, emitting a pervasive stench, with visible excrement everywhere sending shivers down one's spine.

Recalling the days in the arena, Claudius Severus remembered the area in the Roman arena specifically designated for stacking corpses. There, the bodies of fallen gladiators piled up like

Chapter 20

mountains, and the broken limbs were casually thrown into the sewers, attracting reptiles and rodents. When summer arrived, the unbearable stench emanating from there made it hard to endure.

Now, the environment here strangely resembled the underground of the arena. There was a slaughterhouse nearby, and every day butchers threw animal entrails to war dogs. Moments later, you'd see these shattered entrails torn to pieces by the beasts...

Although Claudius Severus and Quintus Marcellus had been granted permission by the local barbarians to no longer be confined in underground dungeons and had found work, Claudius Severus still felt that things were not straightforward. The Gauls might be foolish, but they wouldn't easily trust them. What if the slave brand was intentionally left by Roman spies in advance?

Claudius Severus believed that barbarians were not fools, and a new test was about to come.

Now, he became a link between the two factions, both hoping to gather intelligence about the other through him. The Gauls wanted to know about the internal situation of the Roman legion, while the Roman legion commanders hoped he would infiltrate the barbarians to obtain real intelligence. For Agrippina, Claudius Severus was determined to stand on the side of Rome.

"Those shorties are requisitioning food on our territory again.

Damn it, if it weren't for the southern tribes surrendering to these shorties, we would have trapped them here, with no food, and the Romans would have starved in their camp long ago."

"Yeah, those guys, taking away our things and kidnapping our women. If it weren't for the chief being cautious, I would have rushed into their camp to have a good fight with those shorties. Fortunately, the Germans are coming. I heard there are quite a few of them. Damn it, now we have a chance to slaughter the Romans like livestock."

Having just washed his hands, Claudius Severus heard several Gauls loudly arguing at the tavern, discussing important intelligence about the imminent arrival of the German army.

"Brother, quiet down a bit. I'll handle this."

Facing his companion's impetuosity, Claudius Severus promptly restrained him. Although Quintus Marcellus didn't understand why they weren't going to gather information about the Germans at this moment, as a follower, he knew to act according to Claudius Severus's instructions. They entered the territory of the Gauls, and everything proceeded according to Claudius Severus's plan.

In the tavern, the Gauls continued to talk about the current situation, insulting the Roman legion from the commander to the common soldiers, with no one spared. Claudius Severus remained indifferent, casually reclining by the window, enjoying the rare leisure. Quintus Marcellus stared intently at the Gauls.

Chapter 20

"The German army plans to directly besiege the shorties' camp. They will have no chance of escape. We Gauls have learned the engineering techniques of the shorties. Damn it, by then, we will build a circle of defenses, trap them inside, and then slowly destroy their fortifications with siege weapons."

"That's right, with the Germans coming, our tribe will surely triumph!"

In their excitement, the Gauls continued to discuss the news of the imminent arrival of the German army. However, Claudius Severus was already drowsy, leaning against the window and dozing off.

"Is this guy really not a Roman spy?"

Several Gauls, seeing Claudius Severus's reaction, felt confused and quietly discussed whether they should report back to the chief.

"Wait, let's go and actively ask him about military intelligence, see how he reacts."

"Alright."

The Gauls whispered and approached this outsider. At the same time, Quintus Marcellus remained alert, while Claudius Severus half-opened his eyes, appearing indifferent to everything around him. There was half a bottle of wheat beer on the table.

"Hey, Roman slave, heard that the Germans are coming? Would you be willing to pick up weapons with us, go and chop your former masters? Damn Romans, whatever they did to you before, now we want to massacre them like animals."

The leader of the Gauls spoke first, covered in various animal tattoos with strange ornaments adorning his face, making him appear even more menacing. Claudius Severus woke up in a haze, looking around at the Gauls, one of whom happened to be the barbarian who had beaten him earlier that day. However, at this moment, the Gaul almost wished to tear apart this Roman slave. Yet, the chieftain had commanded that, regardless of whether these two slaves were Roman spies or not, Jurgencus couldn't treat them arbitrarily. How to handle it would depend on the chieftain's decision.

"Claudia Marsala, who do you think you are? We have been earnestly hoping to gain your support here at Three Heads. We hope you can stand on our side. But you keep serving the Senate, causing trouble for Caesar and Pompey. Don't think that without you, Crassus, Caesar, or Pompey can't ultimately triumph."

In the splendid Claudia Marsala mansion, Valerius Aurelius, usually mild-mannered, was furious. He couldn't tolerate having visited multiple times, offering all kinds of benefits, yet this old fool consistently responded with sarcasm, refusing to cooperate. It was as if a clown bowed and scraped before a lady of quality, only to receive disdainful glances. Valerius Aurelius felt ridiculous.

Chapter 20

"Valerius Aurelius, my colleague, my friend. We were once so close, such intimate friends. When you were in trouble, pursued by creditors, I took the initiative to use my wealth to settle those creditors' henchmen for you. When you wanted to pursue Livia but suffered from a lack of property and status, I financially supported you, spoke on your behalf to Livia, making you a couple. But what were our initial ideals? What were we collectively pursuing? The Republic! Rome experienced the monarchy era; everyone knows a country can't go without democracy for a day, and the Senate represents such democracy. Look back, Valerius Aurelius, look at the friendship between us, don't make me draw my sword against you. Don't let your desires cloud your judgment."

Facing Valerius Aurelius's outburst, Claudia Marsala also pleaded with sincerity. However, in this world full of intrigue, who cared about the other's feelings? Desire led people astray, and the environment accustomed them to the status quo, numbing their former ideals and aspirations. When the aroma of wine and the softness of fur eroded one's will, what else could make people reminisce about those times of struggle? The once beautiful vows had long been corroded by money and greed.

"There's no Republic anymore, Claudia Marsala! Now is the era of giants, and Rome's future will belong to one of Caesar, Pompey, or Crassus. The Republic, stop dreaming about it."

Valerius Aurelius continued to shout loudly. The servants outside were already trembling. They didn't know what would happen next. In these days, Rome had witnessed many bloody events. Those so-called democratic elections were filled with violence and bribery behind the scenes. People who stood firm for their beliefs and positions had long been buried beneath the bloodshed.

Throughout Rome, on the surface, everything was calm, but in reality, undercurrents were surging.

"No, I will never compromise, I will fight for the cause of the Republic for a lifetime!"

Claudia Marsala stood up. Her not-so-tall figure seemed like a resilient poplar in its twilight years, weathered on the outside, yet internally devout and steadfast. For the older senators, they were powerless against what was happening in Rome.

"Alright, alright, let's calm down. Let's talk this through, what is democracy?"

Valerius Aurelius suppressed his anger and gradually calmed down. In Rome, politicians spoke like this when discussing practical issues. Sometimes, even in the Senate hall, bloodshed incidents occurred. People gathered for their ideals, but conflicts were inevitable. When conspiracies failed, only bloody open violence remained.

"The Senate represents the Republic. It is the goal countless Romans have fought for."

Claudia Marsala spoke first.

Chapter 20

"Fine, since you say the Senate represents democracy, how much of the Senate's strife in history was caused by unfairness and lack of democracy? Actually, the Senate only represents the interests of the aristocracy. The common people and the equestrian class don't have much say there. Do you agree, my dear friend Claudia Marsala?"

Seeing the older senator's silence, Valerius Aurelius continued questioning.

The Senate has long debated seemingly numerous issues, but in reality, there is only one core question: when faced with affairs, do they prioritize the interests of the nobility or those of the common people and the masses? Valerius Aurelius, my old friend, you claim the Senate is democratic and just, but where does the Senate stand and what are the outcomes when deliberating on matters? Eighty percent of the Senate consists of the nobility, the result is evident. Despite having tribunes to protect the people, their terms last only a year. In such a brief time, how many truly consider the well-being of Rome's commoners?"

Valerius Aurelius relentlessly pressed on, closing in step by step. Claudia Marsala found herself momentarily speechless. This wasn't just a matter of political maneuvering; it was a fundamental question concerning the governance of Roman society and a historical dilemma. One had to admit that Valerius Aurelius made some valid points.

"Well, well, Senator Valerius Aurelius, despite your somewhat valid arguments, the future of Rome cannot be controlled by a minority. It's much better than returning to the monarchy era."

Claudia Marsala still clung to her stance. Since the power struggle between them was neck-and-neck, emotionally, they stood on opposite sides. Thus, they had to rely on debate.

"The times call for heroes, my Claudia Marsala. When Pompey set out to the east, how many voices in the Senate opposed, claiming he was amassing power and threatening the fundamental Roman system with military authority? However, five years later, Pompey not only defeated pirates, opened trade routes, but also conquered numerous tribes and towns in the East. He expanded Rome's territory by a third, doubling the entire financial income of Rome. Imagine such achievements, could the incessant debates in the Senate achieve that?"

Valerius Aurelius spoke with facts, continuing to attack Claudia Marsala's tense nerves.

"History demands continuous development, with changing times, the system also needs to change. Once, Rome was just a city-state, and the Senate republic was enough to handle its affairs. However, after centuries of expansion, Rome has become a world power, and the old system cannot adapt to such a vast nation. Therefore, we need heroes, and Caesar, Pompey, or Crassus are outstanding figures of this era. Whoever brings prosperity and glory to Rome is the master of this age. From the perspective of war, the Senate's system is only suitable for times of peace, but since the founding of Rome, how many years have been peaceful? Almost none. The annually changing consuls cannot cope with such frequent wars. Hence, we had

Chapter 20

Fabius, Scipio, Marius, Caesar, and Pompey. So many facts have proven that Rome needs a change, my friend."

Valerius Aurelius spoke fluently, and after saying all this, Claudia Marsala felt her heartbeat quicken. Although the reality was as he described, it wasn't how reality should be. While war brought enormous wealth to Rome, it also corroded this once thrifty and simple nation. When consuls no longer farmed after their terms, the country had already embarked on the path of greed. Behind extravagance lay crises and the decline of morality.

"Valerius Aurelius, since our views and attitudes are so divergent, I think our discussion today is enough. However, there is one thing I would like to inform you. The Senate has formed a fleet under the pretext of rampant piracy and has entrusted its leadership to Pompey, appointing him as the overall commander of the Roman navy."

Claudia Marsala calmly revealed the latest information to Valerius Aurelius. Yet, this wasn't to have him relay the information to Pompey, nor was it an attempt to win the support of this senator. It was simply a warning from Claudia Marsala to her former friend, indicating that this conflict might not last indefinitely, and the ultimate outcome was unpredictable.

"Are you trying to create a rift between Pompey and Caesar?"

Valerius Aurelius quickly grasped the situation; the Senate was actively trying to exploit the discord between Caesar and

Pompey. They aimed to deepen this division, making Pompey believe that being appointed as the overall commander of the navy was a concession from the Senate, convincing him that the Senate was his true ally while Caesar was not to be trusted.

As public opinion increasingly leaned towards Caesar, the rising star who, with his contributions during his consulship and care for the common people, had garnered widespread support, Pompey, like Sulla surpassing Marius in the past, began to feel deep concern. History might repeat itself, and in this alliance with Caesar, Pompey found it difficult to discern his true allegiance.

"Yes, I'm not worried that you know about these obvious intentions and actions. My old friend, I'm not telling you this to have you turn around and convince Pompey – you lack that ability, and besides, you've already aligned yourself with Caesar. I'm telling you this to make you understand that this struggle is far more complex than it seems on the surface. The Senate plays a crucial role in Rome, and until the very end, no one knows who the victor will be."

Claudia Marsala also calmed down, raising her glass and sipping the red liquid gently. All conspiracies would eventually turn into brutal bloodshed, much like how even the most delicious grapes would be pressed into pulp to become fine wine. Struggles were like that – a harsh process, and it was about who could enjoy the final fruits.

"I'm curious, how did I end up on Caesar's side?"

Chapter 20

The fact that Pompey took command of the Roman navy was beyond Valerius Aurelius's jurisdiction. However, the mention of being on Caesar's side by Claudia Marsala left Valerius Aurelius deeply unsettled. What did this cunning Senate member know?

"Well, since you're pretending not to know anything, let me unveil this layer of hypocrisy. The infamous murder case of Lucius that shook the entire city of Rome was, in fact, orchestrated and manipulated by you. Then, the slave Octavius, whom you personally sent to the gallows, was also released by you. Am I correct?"

"Crying foul and full of deceit. That case had long been concluded by the judiciary; the entire city knows that Lucius's death was orchestrated by Julius himself through his own slave."

Faced with Claudia Marsala's accusations, Valerius Aurelius felt somewhat guilty but still insisted on his viewpoint. However, this seasoned Senate member couldn't help but feel deeply uneasy about how Claudia Marsala knew he stood on Caesar's side. He genuinely wanted to know. Yet, at this moment, revealing his unease and curiosity would only make him appear more vulnerable.

"You don't need to defend yourself further. On the day of the gladiator execution, you bribed the people at the arena. Coincidentally, there was someone of mine present. It's as simple as that."

Claudia Marsala observed Valerius Aurelius, who remained

silent, and emphasized further:

"Later, I started investigating your motives through this incident. Why would a noble with no connection to this matter take such risks to rescue a slave unrelated to him? I followed the leads, searched continuously, and ultimately discovered your plot, Valerius Aurelius. All the crimes, all the evidence, all the conspiracies – they were all masterminded and manufactured by you. You even colluded with Priscilla's daughter to release that criminal, Octavius."

"Enough!"

Valerius Aurelius suddenly roared, infuriated by the realization that despite his meticulously executed actions, his every move had been uncovered. He cursed himself for being careless. Valerius Aurelius felt a profound sense of frustration within.

He had believed everything was concluded, but Livia's concerns were proven right.

He should have heeded this woman's advice, kept a closer eye. Now, Claudia Marsala possessed evidence of his attempts to appease Caesar, while the Senate was working to sow discord between Caesar and Pompey. If Claudia Marsala were to disclose this information to Pompey at this moment, given Pompey's temperament, how would he treat Valerius Aurelius? He could hardly imagine, but simultaneously, he was puzzled – why wouldn't Claudia Marsala reveal the truth to Pompey, knowing the facts? Wasn't she seeking to undermine him and reduce the power of all three factions?

Chapter 20

...

Valerius Aurelius neither admitted nor answered. However, his gaze, his demeanor, had already betrayed him. Claudia Marsala could be sure that her speculations and the evidence she possessed were entirely accurate.

"I won't expose you, my dear friend. It's useless for me to do so. I merely want you to understand that if I truly wanted to crush you, I could have done so already. I've refrained, hoping you'd halt your mad pursuits and return to your true self. Don't let the corrupting wind of concentrated power descend upon Rome again. We are Romans; don't let the corruption of power return."

Claudia Marsala earnestly persuaded Valerius Aurelius in the end.

This time, Valerius Aurelius had failed, utterly. While he might be more cunning and scheming against Caesar, against the core members of the Senate, he was clearly lacking. Yet, the insatiable greed for power was inherent in human nature.

"No, Claudia Marsala, even if you've uncovered all this, based on my association with the Gaius family, Pompey won't suspect my motives. I believe Pompey is not such a narrow-minded person."

Valerius Aurelius defended himself with the little hope he had left. However, he was unaware that Claudia Marsala had acquired even more clandestine information –

"The Gaius family might be just one of the many families with blood ties to Caesar, but the boy named Gaius Octavius has become Caesar's closest confidant, possibly even his adopted son. You cannot deny this, perhaps you are unaware, but the Senate knows, and Pompey might know by now."

Underneath this earth-shattering revelation, Valerius Aurelius's luck seemed feeble and pale. Everything was coincidental, yet when all these coincidences converged, Valerius Aurelius found himself unable to justify his actions.

Afterword

As the intricate web of political intrigue tightens its grip on the characters in "The Song of Rome Volume 2," the layers of deception and clandestine motives become ever more apparent. Claudius Severus, now caught between the Gauls and the Roman legion, finds himself a pivotal link, a pawn in a greater game of intelligence gathering.

Within the political landscape of Rome, Claudia Marsala and Valerius Aurelius engage in a battle of wits, their conflicting ideals and ambitions shaping the destiny of the Republic. As alliances shift and betrayals unfold, the reader is drawn deeper into the heart of power struggles that threaten to unravel the very fabric of Roman society.

The revelation of Valerius Aurelius's intricate plots, his manipulations and collusions, adds a layer of complexity to the narrative. The stakes are raised as secrets are exposed, leaving characters at the mercy of their own choices and the unforgiving tides of Roman politics.

The impending arrival of the German army becomes a focal point, promising a clash that will echo through the annals of history. As the Gauls discuss their plans, and Claudius Severus treads carefully in this volatile environment, the reader is left on the edge of anticipation, eager to witness the unfolding drama that will decide the fate of nations.

In the shadowy corridors of power, Claudia Marsala's plea to Valerius Aurelius resonates, echoing a timeless warning against the corruption of power. The narrative invites reflection on the nature of political machinations, the fragility of alliances, and the moral compass that guides individuals in a world consumed by ambition.

As we delve deeper into the intricate plots and conflicting loyalties, "The Song of Rome Volume 2" becomes a mesmerizing tapestry of history, politics, and human drama. The reader is left yearning for more, eager to turn the pages and discover the twists and turns that lie ahead in this enthralling saga of ancient Rome.

Printed in Dunstable, United Kingdom